The Timekeeper's Tapestry

The
Timekeeper's
Tapestry

Leda Osborne

ARCHWAY
PUBLISHING

Archway Publishing books may be ordered through booksellers or by contacting:

Archway Publishing
1663 Liberty Drive
Bloomington, IN 47403
www.archwaypublishing.com
1 (888) 242-5904

ISBN: 978-1-4808-5140-5 (sc)
ISBN: 978-1-4808-5138-2 (hc)
ISBN: 978-1-4808-5139-9 (e)

Library of Congress Control Number: 2017955094

Print information available on the last page.

Archway Publishing rev. date: 1/8/2018

DEDICATION

This book is dedicated to Rob, Nick and Dan who have loved and supported me through the creative process, and to Patricia and Joyce who have encouraged me to keep writing and to pursue publication. Thank you for your critiques and creative insights. This is also dedicated to my fellow armchair scientists who wish to explore theoretical insights into the mysteries of our existence.

INTRODUCTION

Discussions concerning the nature and structure of time have been going on for as long as man has existed. Is it omnipresent? Can the past be revisited? How is time affected by outside forces such as speed, gravity or simple observation? The questions are as endless as time itself.

For me, time has been a fascination for as long as I can remember. As a child I often dreamt of the day when I would solve its mysteries by building the first time machine. Along with my ability to travel through time, would come the opportunity to "undo" the catastrophic mistakes made throughout mankind's past and thereby help create a world of peace and harmony.

I am many years beyond those dreams of my youth, but a part of me still wishes for that mastery of time. In my book, The Timekeeper's Tapestry, the characters, Blaine Duncan and Penelope Burke, find themselves, through no will of their own, caught up in a thrilling, tragic and sometimes humorous adventure. This sends them both forward and backward through time, as the timekeeper struggles to right a terrible wrong and restore both lost lives and the timeline which was meant to be.

As you read, I hope you will experience some of the fascination I have felt all these years as I have considered all the complexities of time.

CHAPTER 1

THE TIMEKEEPER

There are those, I suppose, who would claim that time, being linear, would not allow for such events as have occurred within my boundaries—those who would declare and defend that events once past, are indeed past without ability to alter, impact, impede, intersect, overlap or in any way manifest themselves in the present. They would be wrong.

The human perspective is extremely limited at best, and woefully failing in awareness and conceptual thinking at worst. That is, at least, within the span of mortality. Therefore, Keepers, such as I, are required to record, sort through and occasionally expose the past to the present and vice versa. Of course, this could not easily be done; I regret to admit, without the compelling emotional offerings, sometimes violent encounters and careless indiscretions that human mortals leave in their wake.

"Who am I?" you might ask. As I have already referred to myself as a Keeper, I will attempt to expand upon that title, for it is as complete a definition as any from your human perspective. I keep the past, present and future, all of time as it were, within the boundaries to which I am assigned. There are others like me with their own boundaries. Don't ask me who they are or who assigned us, for I have no answer for that. I can tell you that a Keeper, such as I, has only one rule. In time, there are no rules. In fact, I find that the more I blend together past, present and future, the more interesting my work becomes. I am somewhat limited by the emotional littering of the human participants within my boundaries and I must sometimes endure long periods wherein nothing noteworthy occurs to present me opportunities for "creativity," if I may put it that way.

In general I find mortals to be petty and self-serving, devoid of imagination and completely limited in their thinking. They are, for all intents and purposes, children, and badly behaved children for the most part. But, on occasion, I have observed those with a greater potential. It is those individuals who make my work most rewarding and satisfying. It is through them that I am able to craft masterpieces of love, justice, fear, honor, courage and destiny. I suppose it may be said that I am an artist, gathering the raw materials of human experience within my boundaries and weaving them together with time to create an intricate tapestry of perceived reality. Nevertheless, I am limited by the independent will of the mortals with whom I must work. Likewise, I am limited by the geographical boundaries to which I am assigned.

Having said that, I suppose I should identify those boundaries. In the late 1600's my boundaries were simply defined as Burkeshire Manor, a sprawling 300 acre estate in what is now called Maine, situated in the area currently known as Machias or Machias Bay, Maine. Though there have been many changes in both the structures and legal boundaries of the estate through the centuries, the original 300 acres remain mine. It is there that our time defying tale begins.

PENELOPE WHITTIER BURKE

The English first became acquainted with this northern territory in 1633, when Richard Vines established a trading-post there. At this time a fierce conflict was going on between France and England, and in the following spring, La Tour, the French commander in the region, made a decent upon it from his seat at Port Royal, killing some of its defenders and carrying the rest away with their merchandise. Attempts were not made again by the French or English for upwards of 120 years.

It was during that time in 1678 Levi Burke, arriving with his young wife, Penelope Whittier Burke, as well as a bevy of builders and servants, laid claim to a 300 acre peninsula in the region. Having acquired substantial wealth in the lumber industry in the area of Massachusetts, at the age of 52 he was now desirous to establish his legacy in the embodiment of Burkeshire Manor. Penelope Burke, at the tender age of nineteen, was early with child when they embarked on this endeavor in early spring.

I observed with little interest that first year as provisional quarters were built, first for Master Burke and his bride, and then for workers and servants. The rush was on to prepare adequate housing before the onset of winter. Penelope's child, a son, was born in the depths of winter and died shortly thereafter with pneumonia, thereby initiating the establishment of a family cemetery near the developing site of the manor. Six additional children were born to the couple over the next decade. Four survived. Penelope and Levi now had a son and three daughters. Three small graves now marked the grounds of the cemetery.

The manor itself, constructed to incorporate native timber, quarried stone and masonry, was majestically situated on a heavily treed bluff, with the windows strategically placed for ample view of the ocean and natural surroundings. The construction of the home and service buildings was finally completed fourteen years after it had begun. By this time I had significantly more interest in the events unfolding at Burkeshire Manor. Specifically, in Penelope Burke and her growing despair.

Burkeshire Manor, upon its completion, was a testament indeed, not only to wealth, but to power and distinction. It was Levi Burke's own creation of rich design and spacious excess. The first floor hosted a grand entry of finest marble, including twin marble columns central to the room. The backdrop to the entry held a sweeping staircase of rich mahogany that wound in a half circle to the second floor. Flanking the entry to the left was the parlor, exquisitely appointed with the finest furnishings money could buy. To the right was the library, which held over two thousand works of fine literature, historical essays, art, and music, including a grand piano. To the rear of the staircase, double doors opened to a grand dining room complete with two imported crystal chandeliers that hung like crowns of royalty over a flawless, twenty-foot-long mahogany table, and chairs of mammoth weight and proportions. Fine works of art filled every wall.

Behind the parlor and to the left of the grand dining room lay a passageway to an enormous kitchen with all the most modern features of the period. At one end of the kitchen was a large larder, including stairs that led down to the food cellar.

The second floor held the master suite, a guest suite and the ladies suite, the latter of which Penelope had chosen to make her own. While she never denied her husband the pleasure of her company when he was home, which was infrequently, she had no wish to occupy the marriage suite while he was away.

The third floor held the nursery and the children's rooms as well as a large play room. All of the staff lived in the staff quarters, which was only a few steps from the main house; however, there were small sleeping quarters off the kitchen, and another small room on the third floor near the children.

Aside from the main entrance, there was a carriageway

entrance on the main floor behind the library and another entrance in the rear of the kitchen.

The manor was completely staffed under the charge of Mr. and Mrs. Wilmington. Mrs. Wilmington instructed four house staff, including the cook, two housekeepers, and Mrs. Burke's personal maid, Chloe. She also kept a record of household needs and supplies. New orders for supplies were given to Mr. Burke upon his departures, and supplies were either sent back via carrier or Mr. Burke brought them back upon his returns.

Mr. Wilmington likewise managed three outside staff in such duties as gardens, care of domestic animals, such as a milk cow, chickens, and horses; care of carriages, firewood, hunting, butchering, structural maintenance and any other request made by Mr. Burke.

One might, upon initial observation, consider despair in such an environment of luxury and ease to be without foundation. Indeed, Levi Burke believed thus. However, having an abundance of temporal and care needs provided at will, is no substitute for love, nor can it dispel loneliness. Penelope Burke was indeed lonely—but not for the love of her husband, who was thirty-three years her senior. It had been a marriage of design arranged by her father, and while Levi had always treated her with kindness, there was no love between them. No, her heart longed for the life she might have had. She dreamed of how she might have been pursued by a handsome young suitor or attended social events with her peers, or might have even been able to take a carriage ride on a sunny afternoon into the town she grew up in. But here at Burkeshire Manor, she, along with her servants, had been cast into the wilderness with no other human contact, except the occasional stranger at the trading post several miles away. Her four surviving children, Alex, Miriam, Darcy and Ingrid were her only loves and she was loved by them.

It was not her despair that drew her to my attention, however. It was, instead, her humble acceptance. She spoke no ill of her husband and made no complaint to her staff or to her children. She did not even complain of her circumstances to Chloe, who had become very dear to her. They were more friends than Mistress and Maid. This is when I decided to step in. Penelope was a rare and special find among the mortals in my boundary. She deserved better, and I decided to weave some happiness into her life.

BLAINE MICHAEL DUNCAN

As I have previously explained, the limited human perspective of linear time is nothing less than vain ignorance. Were it not so, there would be no need for Keepers, such as me. The truth is infinitely more beautiful and affords near limitless possibilities: past, present and future, always there and waiting to be plucked like a prize rose then grafted elsewhere for maximum effect.

I take my work quite seriously, however, for missteps in time could beget catastrophic results. You must know your mortal players intimately so that you may predict with near accuracy their responses. They are, after all, beings of free will. While I am set apart from mortals by immortality and my mastery of time, I am in no way omnipotent. I merely provide individuals with the necessary time. What they create with that time is their own.

Knowing that, allow me to introduce to you the year 2016, and a gentleman by the name of Blaine Michael Duncan. Mr. Duncan arrived within my boundaries in late August that year and I liked him immediately.

As you might imagine, Burkeshire Manor had changed significantly since the year 1678. Few aspects of its original grandeur remained. The original home still stood, though it had fallen into decay, been restored, fallen again and been restored again. It had changed hands many times, and, from time to time, it stood empty for decades. But through these years, the house had remained.

The carriage house had fallen to ruin with only stone rubble to mark its original location. The staff quarters were completely renovated to serve as a guest house, which bore little resemblance to its original form. Plumbing and electricity had been added to both structures. And, of course, there was the cemetery. The three small graves of Penelope's lost children now lay in the company of the remaining occupants of the manor. They were first joined by their father, then by Mr. Wilmington, his wife, and others until, at last, their dear mother took her place at their side, having outlived each of her children and only succumbing at the age of ninety-six.

There were few records left referencing the Burke family

and what little remained was scattered between the public library and long-ago stored documents in the city's land records.

Prior to Mr. Duncan's arrival, the house had once more been vacant for eleven years. For him and his wife, Christina, it had been the find of a lifetime. Married only three years and with no children as yet, they had dreams of converting this historic treasure into both a home for themselves and, eventually, into a bed and breakfast. They took possession of the home on September 1, 2016, and Burkeshire Manor was about to come to life once again. But this time that was truer than ever.

Blaine and Christina stood in what had once been the grand entry of Burkeshire Manor, also known as the great room. The cobwebs hung at every corner. A thick blanket of dust covered every surface leaving visible particles floating in the air that danced in the sunlight which flooded in from the large front windows. Chunks of fallen plaster and other undefinable debris littered the floor here and there.

Christina sighed happily. "It's just perfect."

Blaine slipped his hand over hers. He loved her so much it almost hurt. It was the exact comment he would have expected her to make. In fact, it summed up all the reasons why he loved her. Christina found beauty in everything, from a small child to a raging storm. It was no surprise to him that she would look at the mountain of work ahead of them and find it "perfect." It's the same way she had looked at him with his hidden insecurities, his too tender heart, his clumsy way of expressing himself and a host of other flaws he was certain he had, and still, she found him "perfect." How could he have been so lucky to have won the love of someone like her?

"I'll get our suitcases from the car," he said. "We can set up our bedding in there," he added, pointing toward the old parlor. "It will be like camping indoors. We'll get a good fire going in the fireplace for the night and get to work in the morning."

"Good. We've got two days before the movers get here. We'll need a clean place to put everything. I think nearly everything we own will fit into one or two of these rooms."

All they had brought with them were a few changes of clothing and some toiletries, two pillows, sleeping bags and air mattresses for sleeping, and a couple of bags of easy to prepare groceries from the local market. Everything else was in the mover's van and on its way from Manhattan. They couldn't wait to move into their dream home and had come ahead to prepare the place.

Little had been done to maintain the house and property in recent years. The grounds were severely overgrown and had begun to succumb to the fall season. Though they had arrived at mid-day, the early September air was much cooler than it had been only two weeks earlier. With the house situated on a bluff over the ocean, the chill in the air from the water had cooled the house as well. Though power and water had been turned on to the house days earlier, the heat had not been turned on. Blaine had insisted that the chimneys, all eight of them, be cleaned and inspected before they took possession.

Once everything had been unloaded and a good fire was going, they decided to take what would only be their second tour of the house before they lost the light. Other than the insertion of five bathrooms over the years—two on the main floor, one off the kitchen and one behind the library near to the carriage entry which was now covered parking; two on the second floor, one in the master suite and one in the main hallway; and one in the hallway of the third floor—the basic floor plan of the manor was nearly the same.

"We should take the master suite," Christina said, as they toured the rooms of the second floor. "It has its own bath so we won't need to share with the guests." Breathing out in awe, she moved to the windows. "Just look at this view. You can see for miles across the ocean and into the bay on the left."

Blaine stood gazing with her at the incredible view. As his eyes scanned the expanse before him, he suddenly felt drawn to look right. There, set on the edge of the bluff some fifty yards to the right of the home, lay the old cemetery with maybe fifteen or twenty headstones placed in balance around a single tree. He caught his breath for a moment. He, of course, had known the cemetery was there, but something else had caught his attention.

"What?" Christina asked, noticing that he was not breathing.

"It's nothing. I just thought I saw someone near the tree, but there's no one now. It was probably just a shadow."

"You don't suppose we have ghosts here? That could be really good for business."

Blaine shook his head and smiled at her excitement. "How do you figure?"

Christina ran with the idea. "Just think of the advertising. Not only could people come for the spectacular views and nostalgic setting, but we could advertise the possibility of ghost sightings. It would be great! People would come in droves!"

"Or stay away in droves," he countered. "Not everyone wants a ghostly encounter, you know."

"Maybe," she laughed. "We'll just file the idea away for now."

After completing their tour and making some mental notes on projects to be done, they settled into the now warm parlor, talking long into the night before finally giving in to happy exhaustion and sleep.

SEPTEMBER 1, 1692

Penelope pulled her shawl more tightly across her bosom as the cool September air drifted in from the ocean. She gently pressed her fingertips to her lips in a kiss and then to each of the three headstones of her deceased infants. "Mother loves you, my darlings," she whispered. The afternoon sun was already beginning its decent, withholding the warmth it had offered up only weeks earlier. The vast expanse of ocean before her only deepened the sadness in her heart. She felt particularly lonely today. Mr. Burke had departed this morning for yet another month of business, leaving her alone with the children and staff. He had only been home for two weeks this time. There had been gifts for the children and for her. Alex, now twelve, had received an elaborate model of a sailing ship. Levi instructed Mr. Wilmington to help him put it together. Penelope read her son's thoughts and quietly admonished him not to express them openly. Alex longed for his father's companionship, but kept these feelings to himself. Each of the three girls, ages nine, seven and four, received beautiful dolls to add to their extensive doll collections. They were thrilled. They, unlike Alex, had come to think of their father as the man who brought gifts. They felt little need to establish a bond beyond that. Penelope was quietly grateful that his continued absence had not negatively affected her daughters.

Penelope's gifts were always the same. To dispel some of her loneliness and to occupy her abundance of time, Penelope had taken up painting. She found she had quite a propensity for it. Levi approved of her artistic abilities and always kept her well supplied with oils, canvas, and brushes. He also brought a number of exquisite frames, although Penelope held most of her work to be private and rarely displayed them in the home. Instead, most of her canvasses stood unframed in her private suite. Among the few exceptions was a portrait she had made of her husband on the twelfth anniversary of their marriage. It was displayed in the corridor just outside the master suite. She was pleased that Levi found it impressive. In spite of the circumstances, he had been both kind and generous to her and the children. She was happy to honor him in this way.

Nevertheless, on this day in early September she felt particularly lonely. She moved her gaze from the ocean to the house.

She had come to think of it as a prison from which there was no escape. As her eyes drifted from one feature to the next, they suddenly stopped. There in the window of the master suite she saw the image of a man looking back at her. She blinked, looked again and it was gone. With Mr. Burke having left that morning, there was no cause for any member of the male staff to be in his room.

She quickly returned to the house, entering by the kitchen. Mrs. Wilmington was in the kitchen as was Miss Millie, the cook, who was preparing vegetables for the evening meal.

"Mrs. Wilmington, is Mr. Wilmington in the house?"

"No, Ma'am. He has taken the men out with the wagon for collecting firewood. Would you like me to send for him?"

"Has he taken all the men with him?"

"Yes, Ma'am. Is something wrong?"

Penelope paused a moment. She must have been mistaken. Perhaps she had seen the housekeeper in the window. "No, Mrs. Wilmington. Everything is fine."

"Yes, Ma'am," she said, knowing better than to pursue it. "Can I bring you some tea to warm you? It's a bit chilly out this afternoon."

"Thank you, Mrs. Wilmington. I'll take it in my room."

"Very well, Ma'am."

Penelope went to her room and stood gazing out the window. She had a similar view as the master suite but with a more complete view of the cemetery. Though she now knew there was no evidence to support what she had seen, she was nonetheless certain she had seen a man. He was young, not like Levi, perhaps about her age. Even in the shadow of the window she could see that he was fair. But what could she do? The moment was past and she had no reasonable way to explain it.

There was a knock on the door and Chloe entered, carrying a steaming cup of tea. "Mrs. Wilmington sent me."

"Thank you, Chloe. Please set it on the desk. Will you sit with me awhile?"

"Yes, of course, Ma'am." She sat on the edge of the bed as Penelope took the chair near her easel that held a newly begun painting. There was a moment of silence. Finally, Chloe spoke. "If I may say so, Ma'am, you seem a bit sad as of late."

Penelope flushed and looked at Chloe. "Does it show?" she asked. "I shall have to remedy that."

"May I speak frankly, Ma'am?"

"My dear Chloe, you are quite possibly my only friend. I welcome your thoughts."

"It's not good for you to be shut up in this house all the time. Perhaps Mr. Wilmington could carry you and the children to the trading post for an outing. The children would enjoy it, I'm certain, and the air might lift your spirits."

"Perhaps. I shall suggest it to Mr. Wilmington. The children do need an outing. However, I'm afraid it will take more than a visit with old Mr. Dodd at the trading post to lift my spirits." Penelope reached for her cup of tea and took a sip. She weighed her thoughts a moment then chose her words carefully. "Chloe, have you ever had the sense that you were on a precipice and about to experience something incredible? Something which could change your life forever?"

"How do you mean, Ma'am?"

"I'm not sure I can express it adequately. It's just a feeling…"

"No, Ma'am. I can't say that I have."

Penelope shook her head and suddenly got to her feet. Chloe rose as well.

"Don't give it another thought, dear. I'm just being silly, I'm sure. I believe I'll take some time at the easel before dinner. Will you see to the children? They should be attending to their lessons. Thank you, Chloe."

Penelope picked up a brush and turned to her canvas. It was a view of the house from the location where she had been this afternoon in the cemetery. She tried to push away her thoughts of strange men appearing in windows and lost herself in her work. There was no need to work from actual view. She had seen this view of the house so frequently, she could work from memory. She was uncertain how much time had passed when she heard Mrs. Wilmington at the door announcing dinner was served.

As she tidied her hands in the wash basin, she thought how Chloe was probably right. She did spend too much time locked away in this house. Her mind was beginning to play tricks on her, seeing a man who couldn't possibly be there, and imagining her life was about to change. Nothing had changed in fourteen years. How could it possibly change now? Perhaps she would take a carriage ride with Mr. Wilmington and the children.

At least it would be a change of scenery and that was about as much change as she dared hope for. She continued to silently chide herself as she descended the grand stairway and joined her children in the dining room.

CHAPTER 2

SEPTEMBER 4, 2016

By the time the movers left, Christina and Blaine were exhausted. They had worked alongside the two men carrying kitchen items to the kitchen, bedroom items to the master suite on the second floor, and living room items to the parlor. Though the moving van had barely been large enough to contain their belongings, the house seemed comically bare once everything had been placed in the appropriate rooms. As they observed the huge discrepancy between their belongings and the available space, they both burst into hysterical laughter.

"I believe we have some shopping to do, Ma'am. Shall I fetch the carriage 'round?" Blaine bowed from the waist as though he were the loyal servant.

"Perhaps in the morning," she replied with as much majesty

as she could muster. Then she added, "My royal ass is whooped."
That sent them both into new fits of laughter as they sank onto
their too small sofa in the parlor.

"Well, give it a year," Blaine said, still smiling. "She'll look
as good and she did in her youth."

"Better," Christina said.

"So, you're not sorry yet?"

"Sorry! Oh, no. I think it's the most wonderful thing we've
ever done. No, Blaine, I'll never be sorry. In fact, I want you to
promise me that no matter what happens we will never leave
here. Not ever. Will you promise me that?"

Blaine took her in his arms and kissed her tenderly. "I
promise," he said. "We'll never leave here."

In three months, by December 1st, they had managed to
properly furnish the parlor with period pieces from the sev-
enteen hundreds. The once marble floors and pillars of the
great room had long ago been replaced with first granite tiles
and later with more affordable fine wood floors. The Duncans
now hired a team to restore the floors to their polished oak
condition. Oak veneer was applied to the twin pillars to tie
them to the floor. Three large sculpted rugs lay beneath two
large French provincial sofas, one on either side of the pillars,
and the third rug lay beneath a mahogany hotel desk they
had found at one of the many antique shops in the area. Two
round Duncan Phyfe tables holding large silk bouquets flanked
the desk. Winged-back upholstered chairs and tea tables were
placed near the sofas. The sweeping staircase had been the one

feature of the home that had held up remarkably well. All that was required was some light restoration of the mahogany banister and the replacement of only a few steps. The steps were then given a complimentary dressing of carpet that tied them to the rest of the room. The blending of woods and periods lent an eclectic air to the room, but Christina felt that it would be inviting to most tastes. Blaine thought that most of their guests probably couldn't tell one period from another anyway, and the intent would be lost on them. In either case, they both agreed that the finished product was breathtaking.

The library shelves had been sanded, cleaned and polished. Neither Christina nor Blaine believed that paint had any place on fine woods. The shelves had been better than half stocked with current literature, historical literature of the area of Maine, and some classic CD's and DVD's. They hoped to acquire more books as they went along. The room also held three computer tables that would someday hold three computers, and a child's corner hosting a small table and chairs with crayons, markers, coloring books and story books. Throughout the room in appropriate locations sat recliners, and other comfortable seating.

The kitchen had been stocked with the appropriate amount and size of cookware, serving dishes, linen, water and wine glasses and more. The dining room had yet to be furnished along with all of the second and third floors.

In spite of the amount of work yet to be accomplished, Blaine and Christina were pleased with what had been achieved so far. They had given themselves one year to be ready for guests. It looked as though they would reach that goal. Though the bedrooms would be less work than the main floor had been, there was still the outside grounds to consider. Winter had made it impossible to address that project for now; however, there was still ample to do inside until spring. At some point, probably after they had opened for business, they had hopes of turning the guest house into their own private quarters and renting out the master suite. Until then, it had become a bit of a storage shed and workshop for restoring old furniture they had purchased for the house.

DECEMBER 20, 2016

I would like to reiterate at this time that I do not control events within the mortal realm. However, I do, being fully aware of past present and future, know what is coming, barring any mishaps from me or any mortal within my boundaries. Please, therefore, do not think me harsh or hold me accountable for these events. They are not within my abilities to control. Nevertheless, it was due to these events that I chose Blaine's life and time as the one most appropriate to assist me in brightening Penelope's life. Furthermore, Penelope, if her heart leads her as I think it will, may also be Blaine's salvation.

Having said that, let us observe the events as they are about to unfold for Blaine Duncan on this December 20, 2016.

Blaine stoked the small fireplace in the guest house, trying to push back the winter cold that had settled in. He had been working all morning, sanding down a wardrobe that, when redone, would go into the second suite, formerly known as the ladies suite, which Penelope Burke had occupied.

Christina had taken their four-wheel-drive suburban into town to buy additional supplies for the job. Approximately ten inches of snow had accumulated in the last two days and although the roads had been plowed, the temperature had dropped to the mid-teens, and ice had become a focus of concern. Though no further snowfall was expected that day, the sky was filled with churning gray clouds that boiled their way across the sky, driven by the constant wind off the ocean. Even at mid-day, the light was dim. Occasional heavy gusts of wind pushed against the windows of the shop, rattling a loose pane. With each of these heavy gusts, the smoke from the fire pushed through the poorly insulated door of the fireplace and billowed into the room. Though these occasional puffs of smoke had begun to irritate Blaine's eyes, it was too cold to open the door or a window. As he worked, Blaine began to feel an uncomfortable and disconcerting sense of dread. He couldn't explain it. Perhaps it was the exceptionally gray day that was weighing on him, though he couldn't recall ever having been so influenced by the weather before this. Nevertheless, his sense of foreboding continued to grow. He wished Christina would return. Her presence could outshine any gray day, and banish the blues with a gentle word or smile. He tried to push the dark feeling away by focusing on the work he was doing, and decided he would suggest an evening out when Christina returned.

As if on cue, he heard the low rumble of her vehicle and the crunch of frozen snow under the tires. He set aside the sander and zipped into his parka, preparing to step outside to help her unload supplies.

Once outside, however, the nagging sense of dread quickly leaped to genuine fear and rising panic. Instead of seeing the suburban pulling up to the house, he saw a dark blue sedan with white lettering on its side which read Machias Police Department. A uniformed officer was stepping out of the vehicle and walking toward Blaine. The solemn look on his face said things that Blaine was already praying he wouldn't have to hear. The officer stopped about two feet in front of Blaine and extended his hand as he introduced himself.

"Mr. Duncan?"

Blaine nodded, without speaking.

"I'm Officer Rush."

Blaine didn't take his hand. The officer let it fall to his side.

"I'm afraid there's been an accident," the officer said.

Blaine swallowed hard. In the space of only two seconds he envisioned all the possibilities of what he was about to hear. None of the possibilities felt good. Possibility number one: she was mildly injured and he could go down to the hospital and pick her up after she was checked out by the doctors. Possibility two: she was seriously injured and could only come home after some time in the hospital. Possibility three: no…he wouldn't go there. The officer was speaking again.

"If you'll come with me, Mr. Duncan, I'll take you to her."

Blaine didn't move and had not yet spoken. "He wouldn't be taking me to her if she were dead," he thought.

"We should leave now," Officer Rush was saying.

Blaine nodded again, following him to the police vehicle and getting into the passenger side. As they pulled onto the road toward town, he finally found his voice. "Is she okay?" he asked.

"You'll have to speak to the doctor about that, Mr. Duncan. I'll have you there in less than five minutes."

Blaine knew that Officer Rush was not going to tell him any more. They rode silently until they reached the hospital. As Blaine got out of the vehicle, Officer Rush said, "I'll be here for the next hour or so when you need a lift back."

His voice was compassionate. That was not a good sign. Blaine rushed into the emergency entrance. He told the entry nurse his name and was immediately taken to the third-floor ICU. As they stepped off the elevator, they were met by another nurse who dismissed the first nurse and then brought Blaine into Christina's room where they met with the doctor. While the doctor attempted to introduce himself, Blaine ignored him for the moment and rushed to Christina's bedside. Her eyes were closed. The entire right side of her face was scraped and badly swollen. Her right hand was bandaged to the elbow. Her hair was matted with dried blood. She was breathing, but it seemed to be difficult for her. Blaine wondered why she wasn't on a breathing tube or any other type of electronic assistance. In fact, the only monitor displaying anything was a heart monitor.

All the other surrounding equipment was dark. The doctor surmised the questions in his mind.

"Mr. Duncan, your wife has suffered a substantial head injury. The pressure from the internal swelling and bleeding is growing by the minute. I'm afraid there's no time to..."

"No!" Blaine shouted. "You have to do something!"

"I can assure you we've done all we can. We'll be just outside," he added, ushering the nurse out with him.

Blaine realized that he had just been given the last minutes he would ever have with his wife. Three short years; that's all they'd had together. They had been the happiest years of his life, and now, without warning, it was all about to end. He buried his face in her neck and sobbed. "Don't leave me, Christina. I can't do this without you. Please don't go."

A soft moan from Christina caused him to pull back to look at her.

"Christina? That's right, baby. Come back to me."

Her eyes fluttered open with great effort. "Blaine," she managed in a soft, barely audible whisper. "Remember your promise. Never leave." Her eyes began to close again.

"No! Don't leave me."

Without opening her eyes, she whispered, "She... can help you. I love you."

The sudden constant beep of the heart monitor told him what he already knew. She was gone. A series of disjointed thoughts raced through his mind. "No. This can't be real. How can she be gone? I need her. We haven't finished the manor.

What about our dream?" He tried to shake her gently awake. "Please don't leave me. Wake up, Christina. Wake up." All the while, in spite of his pleas, he knew it was too late. A nurse quietly walked into the room, turned off the beeping monitor, and quietly walked out again. Blaine knew they were giving him a few minutes in private to gather himself. He wasn't sure how long he sat by her side, holding her hand. After what seemed like twenty or thirty minutes, but was, in reality only ten, he got to his feet, kissed her softly on the lips and walked out.

True to his word, Officer Rush was waiting in the corridor near the nurse's station when Blaine left the room. The doctor had offered the use of the hospital's counseling staff if he felt like talking to someone, but Blaine had refused. The nurse had given him a phone number to call when he was ready to make plans for Christina's remains and offered her condolences one last time.

When Officer Rush saw that the staff had completed their details with him, he walked up to Blaine and simply said, "My shift ended 20 minutes ago. Can I buy you a drink?"

A drink sounded good to Blaine, but he didn't want to be in a crowd. "How about I fix you one at my place?"

"Deal. I'm Jack. Jack Rush."

"Blaine." Blaine said, although he knew that Officer Rush already knew that.

Jack drove them both back to the house. There was only light talk. It occurred to Blaine on the way that he and Christina had not yet given the place a name. Probably the first of many things he would find himself wishing they had done together.

Jack followed Blaine in through the kitchen entrance and sat at a large table as Blaine pulled out a bottle of Jack Daniels and two glasses before joining him. Jack was a little older than Blaine. Maybe 10 years. He looked to be in his mid-40s. Blaine poured them both a healthy shot, then drank his down in one gulp.

"It's a hard thing, I know," Jack said. "I lost my wife two years ago to breast cancer. Yeah, damn hard."

"Sorry to hear that," Blaine said, refilling both their glasses.

"It's a helluva thing to have to tell another man. Coming here today, well, it's a part of my job I wish I never had to do."

Blaine could hear the sympathy in his voice. He was glad he had come to share a drink. He hadn't wanted to walk back in this house alone. Not yet.

The two of them sat for nearly an hour as Blaine talked about the plans he and Christina had made for this place. Though Jack called it quits after the third drink, he stayed and listened as Blaine poured out their story. As his story brought him to that first night they had slept in the parlor, he told Jack how she had made him promise they would never leave here. That suddenly brought his mind back to the hospital room where she lay dying. He thought of the same last words she had said to him, "Remember your promise. Never leave." Suddenly he wanted, needed to be alone.

"Look, Jack, thanks for being here man, but I think I need some time."

Jack understood. "No sweat, but if it's all the same to you, I'd like to stop by again just to see if you're all right."

"Yeah, thanks."

The two men shook hands and then Blaine was alone. Carrying the half-empty bottle of Jack Daniels with him, Blaine climbed the stairs to the master suite. The bed was still unmade. Christina's nightgown lay across the foot of the bed. A picture of the two of them at their wedding sat on the night table near the bed. The alcohol had already made him fuzzy and drowsy. He sat on the edge of the bed, bottle still in hand. He took another long swig, but the loneliness he felt could not be drowned. He knew he could not sleep in this room tonight. He headed for the stairs, intending to sleep in the parlor instead, but only made it as far as the top step then sank down to the floor. He set the bottle beside him with his feet resting on the second step. He could not hold back the tears any longer. With his head buried in his hands, great sobs shook his whole body and he wept until he fell into an alcohol-induced sleep at the top of the great sweeping stairway.

CHAPTER 3

DECEMBER 20, 1692

Levi had returned home that morning. Mr. Wilmington had cut a beautiful tree for the Christmas holiday. He was busy setting it up in the parlor while Mrs. Wilmington and the staff were collecting all of the ornaments and other decorations from their storage place in the attic and carefully carrying everything downstairs. The children and Mr. Burke had gathered in the parlor to begin decorating the tree. Penelope was dressing in her suite and preparing to join them. Once the tree had been set up and all the decorations had been deposited in the parlor, all the servants retired to the kitchen for their evening meal. The Burke family had already eaten. Penelope had been happy for Levi's return, more so for the children than herself. It was a holiday after all. She felt the family should be together.

As she stepped out of her suite and moved to the stairway, she suddenly stopped. Before her, sitting at the top of the stairs, sat a man with his back to her. Beside him on the floor was a bottle of whiskey. He had not seen nor heard her, for he did not turn around. His face was buried in his hands and he was weeping inconsolably. Though she was naturally startled, she was not afraid. His hair was fair and his clothing, well, it was peculiar, yet she was calm. She knew this was the man she had seen in the master suite window, looking down at her a few months earlier. She was sure of it.

Compassion filled her heart as she heard him weeping. She took a step toward him and reached out her hand, but it fell to nothing. He was just gone. She examined the floor where he had been sitting. All seem normal at first, but then she saw a ring of moisture where the bottle had been. She touched it with her fingers and brought her fingers to her nose. There was the distinct odor of alcohol.

The range of emotions that filled her were first relief that she had not imagined him the first time, then wonder. How could this be? How could a man suddenly appear in such a place of isolation, not once, but twice? How could she see and hear him if he were a specter? How could he vanish before her very eyes and yet leave behind visible traces that he had been there? Certainly he must be real to do such things. Who was he? Why was he here? Why was he weeping so? Then, there was also the sense of excitement. What could this mean for her? Would he come again? Would they speak? The possibilities raced through her mind. And then, finally, concern. Had this loneliness and isolation taken its toll on her mind? Was she losing touch with reality and envisioning people who weren't there? She shuddered at the thought. Suddenly, Mrs. Wilmington's voice pierced her thoughts.

"Ma'am, the master and the children are requesting you join them," she said, looking up from the bottom of the steps.

"Yes, of course, Mrs. Wilmington. I shall be there directly." Penelope took a deep breath to compose herself; then went down the stairs to join her family.

DECEMBER 21, 2016

Blaine awoke early the next morning with an all-over ache from sleeping on the stairs. His mouth felt like cotton. His head ached and his eyes were red from both tears and alcohol. His first thought was how lucky he had been to not go tumbling down the steps and break his neck, but as he began to recall the previous day, his next thought was that he wished he had.

He dragged himself to his feet and headed for the shower in the master suite. As he passed by the bed, Christina's nightgown still lay across the foot of the bed, mocking him. He walked past, stripping off his clothes as he went. Turning on the shower, he stepped in, letting it beat down on him until he began to feel awake and somewhat human again. Even then, he stood there for a long time until the water began to turn cold. Finally he shut off the water and stepped out. He put on clean jeans and a sweatshirt, wondering all the while what he was going to do next. He just knew he had to keep moving, because if he stopped he might never move again.

He checked through the pocket of his dirty jeans and came up with the card he had been given by the nurse at the hospital. According to her, at least as much as he actually heard, the man on this card could help him "take care" of Christina, whatever that meant. He read the name on the card. Ben Jacobson. Under his name it read "Parker's Funeral Home." Apparently Ben Jacobson was not the owner, or at least not the original owner of Parker's Funeral Home. He carried the card to the kitchen and set it on the table while he brewed a pot of strong black coffee. He rummaged through a small cupboard that held first-aid supplies and found some ibuprofen for his headache and took two. When he glanced at the clock on the wall, it read 8:10. He didn't know what kind of hours one kept at a funeral home, but he supposed it was probably like a bank, ten to four, unless, of course, if they had a funeral or something. He downed two cups of coffee while his mind rambled on aimlessly. He didn't even know what to say to Ben Jacobson when he called. Something like, "Hello, my wife is dead. What do I do now?" He'd never been through anything like this before. A trained eye would have recognized that Blaine was still in shock. The random, nonsensical thinking, the resistance to real emotions this morning, which constituted denial. What were the steps again? Anger, denial, depression, bargaining, acceptance; he had a long way to go.

Blaine began to think of Christina's last words to him.

"Remember your promise. Don't leave." He thought of their first night here when he'd made that promise. Could he do that? Stay here without her? Right now that seems like an impossible expectation, but part of him said, "This was our dream." Fulfilling that dream seemed like the only way to hold onto her right now. And, they did have their own cemetery. She could be right there with him. This is where she wanted to be forever.

The tears began to burn his eyes once again, but he wouldn't allow himself to break down. He went to the phone and dialed Parker's Funeral Home. It was answered on the third ring. "Ben Jacobson, please."

For the next thirty minutes Blaine and Ben discussed preparations for Christina's funeral. "No one has been buried in the Burkeshire Cemetery for more than 200 years," Ben told him, "but I can't see any reason why your wife can't be buried there. I'll make arrangements with the county." Today was Tuesday. The burial was planned for Saturday. "Would you like an announcement in the paper?"

Blaine thought about that. They were new to the community. They knew few people and none of them very well. Still, he thought her parents would appreciate something. "You write it, okay?"

"I'd be honored. I just need a few facts from you."

Blaine's next call was the hardest. Christina's mother answered the phone. Through many tears on both ends of the call, the sad story was told. Her parents would be there on Friday.

Blaine's parents were in Europe for the winter, but even if they were stateside, he doubted if they could be troubled from their busy schedules. They rarely spoke with him. The wall had been built years ago when Blaine had denounced their self-righteous, elitist attitudes. He felt that their wealth, and consequently his, did not make them any better than anyone else, and that people should be defined by their character and their worthy contributions to society, not by their bank balance. He did not call.

Over drinks the previous night, Jack Rush had explained that Christina's car had been towed to Riley's auto repair in Machias. Blaine called to provide insurance information. Chuck Riley conveyed his condolences and told him he'd get the repairs done and the car back to him within three weeks. Meanwhile, Blaine had his Chevy three-quarter ton. They had purchased it for hauling their furniture finds, and so each of them would have a vehicle.

By the time he'd made all the necessary calls, it was past noon and he felt a rumble in his stomach. With only two cups of coffee that morning, he was hungry. He realized he hadn't eaten since yesterday morning, more than 24 hours ago. He prepared a couple of eggs and toast with all the enthusiasm of a pre-programmed robot, then ate with even less enthusiasm, but it stopped the rumbling.

For the next hour or so Blaine wandered from room to room on the main floor looking at all they had accomplished in only a few months. Each room held a dozen memories of talk, laughter and tenderness they had shared while they worked. But each room also held a glaring emptiness without her in it. He had been without her for less than a day and the loneliness was almost more than he could bear.

The loud chime of the front doorbell so startled him that he gasped. When he opened the door he was glad to see Jack Rush, out of uniform, standing there. Blaine didn't want to be alone and Jack had been good company the day before. "Hey, come in," he said.

"Are you sure?"

"Yeah, yeah I was just thinking; I was getting tired of talking to myself." He laughed but it didn't come out as convincingly as he had intended. Jack pretended not to notice. He took in the view of the lavish great room. "Well, well. You've done a heckuva job on this place. When I heard you folks had bought her, I wasn't sure she was worth saving. Glad to see I was wrong."

"Well, I'm just the labor. All the design stuff was Christina. She's always had a flare."

Blaine gave him a brief tour of the library and parlor. "You've already seen the kitchen," he said, as they seated themselves in the same chairs they had occupied last night.

"I saw Ben Jacobson this morning," Jack said. "He told me of your plans for Saturday. Does that mean you'll be staying?"

"Guess so. I know that's what she wanted."

"Glad to hear it. You know, I know that now isn't the best

time, but when you're ready, there's folks in town who are willing to pitch in and help."

"How would you know that? This just happened yesterday."

"You know how it is. Small town, local cop, word gets around. There's a lot of good folks here."

"Well, I'll keep it in mind. Thanks." Then he added, "You know, I don't mean to sound ungrateful, but you don't need to check up on me. I mean, it's tough, but I'll be okay."

"I know you will. Besides, my visit isn't just to check up on you. Ben sent me with some papers you'll need to sign." He reached inside his jacket and pulled out some papers he had rolled into his pocket. "It's just some legal stuff—routine. I'll just leave them with you. All except one; you'll need to sign it now. If you're wanting to bury your wife in the estates cemetery, we'll need to get a grave dug before Saturday. If you've got any family coming, you'll probably want to have it done before they get here."

"I hadn't thought of that. You're right, of course. Her mother probably couldn't handle watching that done." He skimmed the document authorizing the dig and prep, and signed it at the bottom, handing it back to Jack. "I really do appreciate your help, Jack."

"Well, like I said, I've been through this myself."

Blaine walked him out of the kitchen door and the two men parted with a hearty handshake and pats on the shoulder. Blaine liked him. He knew Jack wasn't just there out of duty, but that he really seemed to care, and, more importantly, understand. He was grateful.

The next few days were a blur. The cemetery crew arrived the next morning with a plow and a backhoe loaded on a trailer. The plow first cleaned the snow from the large area around the house and a twelve foot wide path to the cemetery itself. Another large area was cleared in an unused portion of the small cemetery before digging began. By afternoon the grave had been dug and prepped with an appropriate liner and draped support for the casket.

Blaine watched from the window of the master suite. It was all too real and too dreamlike at the same time. He didn't want to be there yet. He was not ready to choose a headstone yet either. He decided to attend to that at a later date. Since they were new in town, he did not expect many to attend. Perhaps Jack, and those at the funeral home, and her parents. She had no siblings. He was sorry for her parents that there would be so few, but there was nothing he could do.

Jim and Caroline, Christina's parents, arrived on Friday late morning. Blaine met them at the airport and brought them home. Since the master suite was the only partially furnished bedroom, he brought their bags up there. He would sleep in the parlor.

The three of them talked long into the night, sharing stories of Christina's life with her family and with Blaine. Finally, Blaine shared her desire to never leave here and how she had made him promise, then reminded him of that promise before she died.

No one even remembered that it was Christmas Eve. The

next day, Christmas Day, the funeral was to be held at noon. Jim, Caroline and Blaine glumly prepared themselves, dressing for the occasion even though they would be alone.

At eleven o'clock Ben Jacobson and Jack Rush arrived. Jack wore his uniform because he didn't own a suit. As Blaine welcomed them in and introduced them around, Jack said, "You might want to clear a space on the kitchen table. You're going to need the room."

"I don't understand. What for?"

In answer to his question, the sound of vehicles reached the house. Looking out the front window, Blaine saw car after car rolling in behind the hearse and, one by one, fill up the large area that had been cleared by the plow driver. He had apparently been making a parking spot. There must have been 30 cars by the time they stopped coming.

"I don't understand. It's Christmas day. Who are all these people?"

Jack slapped him lightly on the back. "I told you we had some good folks in this town. It was their idea, not mine. And you can bet the women will be bringing plenty of good food with them."

Blaine was stunned. Caroline began to cry. Jim and Jack started directing the women with food to the huge kitchen. Soon the large entry was filled with people. Beautiful bouquets and dozens of cards were set on the entry desk and surrounding tables.

Becky McCutchen and Jed Wilkes, from the two antique

shops where they had purchased many of their furnishings, were there. Other merchants, whose faces Blaine recognized, but did not know by name, were also there, as well as countless faces he had never seen before. He was deeply touched by the outpouring of support. He looked at Jack who was smiling like a kid on Christmas morning. How appropriate.

While the crowd bustled inside, the funeral home crew quickly and quietly worked outside, carrying the casket to the grave and setting up chairs around the site. Additional flowers were brought to cover the casket. Three chairs were placed at the head of the casket for Blaine, Jim and Caroline.

Shortly before noon Ben Jacobson requested that the guests make their way to the graveside. Though the temperature was near freezing, no one complained. Everyone proceeded in a reverent manner to their places beside the grave. Jim, Caroline and Blaine arrived last.

Ben Jacobson delivered a beautiful service, after which one guest step forward with a violin to accompany the gathering as they sang, "Nearer My God to Thee." The family was offered the opportunity to speak, but both Jim and Caroline were too overcome and declined. Blaine stood in silence for a moment in an effort to compose himself. Finally, he spoke. "I can't express to all of you how touched we all are by your love and support. I know Christina must feel the same. I guess I just want to say thank you. All of you."

He started to sit down, then thought better of it, and said, "Shall we all go inside?"

With that, everyone quietly filed back to the house—everyone, except Blaine. He lingered a few moments near Christina's grave. "I guess you were right about this place. This is our home. A lot of people went out of their way to say that today. I wish you were here to see that. Well, I guess you probably are. I love you, Christina. I will always love you. And, I will always be here."

It was nearly 3 o'clock when the last of the guests left. Although Blaine had been grateful for their support, he was glad to have the house to himself again. Well, almost to himself.

Sunday he saw Jim and Caroline to the airport where they said a heartfelt goodbye. "You know you are always welcome in our home," Caroline said. "You are family. The only family we have now."

"Thank you. I feel the same." And he meant it.

CHAPTER **4**

For the next several days Blaine was alone in the house. Even Jack stayed away. He tried to spend time in the workshop on the wardrobe he had been sanding the day of the accident, but he found it hard to feel any motivation. Yes, he had made the decision to stay, but his wounded heart was still too new. Right now it was still a challenge to get up in the morning, eat at least once a day and even remember to breathe. Along with his decision to stay, he had also made a decision not to turn to alcohol for relief, like that first night. He knew that in time the pain would soften a little and life would be more bearable. It just seemed like that was still so far away.

MARCH 12, 2017

By March 12, 2017, Blaine had finished all the furniture for the second suite. Before he could move it in, however, he needed to finish papering the one wall. Christina had ordered the paper for that room before the accident. The other three walls had been painted an eggshell blue.

After sanding down and prepping the fourth wall, Blaine decided he would spend that evening getting the paper up. The walls, of course, were nearly 11 feet high in this old house and not an easy task for one person. He managed a few strips before he ran into trouble. As he stood on the ladder to first attach the upper portion, the lower part of the strip would flutter and stick where it didn't belong. Off the ladder now and trying to correct the lower portion of the strip, the upper portion was suddenly loosened and floated down over him like a blanket.

"This was so much easier with two people," he muttered. "Where are you when I need you, Christina!" He almost yelled. His frustration grew to anger incredibly fast. "I need you!" He was now yelling. "Why did you leave me? Why?" Like a reflex, he slammed his fist into the wall, then whirled in a circle, kicking his foot through the wall, below where he had broken through with his fist. The old plaster crumpled away at the point of impact. He didn't care. He slumped to the floor and began sobbing again for the first time since the night of her death.

When he had cried himself into a numb calm, he looked at the damage he had done to the wall. In his sitting position on the floor he had a better view of the damage made by his foot. The hole was much larger than the one made by his fist. But it was not the hole itself that caught his attention; behind the crumpled plaster, inside the wall, he saw something. He scooted closer, using his finger to pluck at the plaster and open the hole even wider. Yes, something was definitely in there. As he continued to open the wall larger and larger he could see the hidden objects. They were canvas paintings and there were many. He pulled them out carefully, one by one, and laid them face-up on the floor around him. The subject of each piece was the manor, the cemetery, this house, both inside and out, the grounds, the guest house and more. But what was more interesting was that these paintings were clearly done in the original days of the manor. Each painting had a signature in the lower right corner. Penelope Whittier Burke. And under each signature, was a number.

As fascinating as all this was, it was the content of each painting that nearly sent him reeling. In each painting—every one—was a man. Not just any man. It was him, Blaine Duncan!

Blaine was dumbfounded. What does this mean? How could this be? He looked again at the numbers beneath each signature. He wondered if they were in order. He lined them up against the wall in numerical order. He had been right. The numbers went from 1 to 33.

He looked closer at number two. His blood chilled. It was an interior painting of him sitting at the top of the stairs weeping, just as he had done the night of the accident. There sat a bottle on the floor beside him. And behind him, oh my God, behind him stood a woman who could only be Penelope Burke, dressed in period clothing appropriate to the original house, reaching out to touch him with a look of compassion on her face. His eyes moved to number one. It was a view of the house from the cemetery. In the foreground, once again, Penelope Burke stood gazing up at the house. And there, in the window of the master suite, stood Blaine looking down at her. His mind quickly raced back to the day Christina and he had stood at the window of the master suite looking out. He remembered that he had, for just a moment, thought he'd seen a woman near the tree in the cemetery and then decided it must have been a shadow. Now he wasn't so sure. There it was, in front of him. But that was impossible. Penelope Burke had been dead for more than 260 years. He looked at the other paintings. Nothing seemed familiar. He wondered why. And why was Christina not shown in the window beside him? Did he really have a ghost in his house? No. That didn't make sense either. These paintings were clearly as old as the house itself, and he had never heard of a ghost that created works of art. And if these paintings were by the hand of Penelope Burke, how could they depict events that wouldn't happen for nearly 300 years? There was no explanation. At least, there was no explanation he could imagine. Not yet.

He carefully collected each painting and brought them one by one to the master suite. Without knowing exactly why, he went down to the shop and collected enough hangers for each picture. He returned to his room and carefully hung each one in order around his room where he could see each of them from the bed.

I watched this with some delight. Blaine was curious and his mind was open to possibilities. I knew I had chosen well. Penelope, too, was open to possibilities. Each was so far beyond their peers in the mortal realm. So much more willing to accept what was normally beyond comprehension. How delightfully refreshing their minds were. All that I waited for now was for Blaine to put the next piece together. I knew it would not be long. And, of course, I knew he would.

For the next two nights Blaine lay awake in his room studying each painting. He had narrowed down a short list of certainties from which to build a hypothesis. One: he was in each painting and Penelope Burke was also in many. Two: the background of each painting clearly depicted the home and the grounds in the distant past. Even the interior painting showed furniture and artwork that did not exist in the house today. In painting number one, the cemetery showed only three small gravestones. In painting number two at the top of the stairs, the carpet was different than what existed today. In the background were pieces of art on the wall that Blaine had never seen. What did all this mean?

Blaine concluded that it meant this: In each painting, Penelope Burke or her spirit had not come here to see him, but it must have been him that somehow, some way, had moved back through time, if only for a moment, to a living Penelope Burke, where she had seen him and recorded the event on canvas. He could think of no other explanation. Even then, he knew he'd have to test his theory. But how? He concluded that the paintings had been done in the order they occurred, both because seeing her in the cemetery had occurred before he was depicted weeping on the stairs, and because the paintings had been numbered in that order. Therefore, his next step was painting number three. This painting was clearly done in what he called the second suite, where he had found the paintings sealed away in the wall. He could tell by the window placement and the general shape of the room. In this painting he was depicted standing with his back to the window, looking as though he were speaking to someone in the room. Another aspect of each painting, that supported the theory that he had traveled back through time, was his clothing. In spite of the fact that each painting depicted the manor in its early days, Blaine's clothing was always the clothing of his day, not hers. In painting number three, the room was completely and beautifully furnished in the decor of the day. Blaine decided that this painting depicted the next time they would be together in time. He reasoned that it would most certainly happen, because the painting had already been made.

The next evening Blaine dressed in the clothing he was wearing in painting number three. He slowly walked down the hall to the second suite where the door was closed. He hesitated. A slight tingling sensation spread through his body. He raised his hand and knocked on the door. At about the same time his head started swimming. He heard a woman's voice calling, "Enter." He gently pushed the door open, stepping into Penelope Burke's private bedroom. Everything went dark and he felt himself collapse to the floor.

CHAPTER 5

MARCH 13, 1693 (EVENING)

Penelope gasped at the sight of her fair-haired young man entering her room, then collapsing in a faint to the floor. She rushed to close the door behind him, checking the hallway first to make certain no one had seen him enter. Wearing her bed dress, she quickly fetched a shawl to cover herself, then carefully knelt beside him on the floor. He was still completely out. She slowly reached out her hand and held it just above his chest. She could feel his body heat rising to her palm. "So," she whispered quietly, "you are not a ghost, but a living man." She lowered her hand onto his chest. "A spirit is not solid to the touch as you are. Perhaps now we shall discover who you are and why you have come to me."

She fetched a cloth, dipped it in the wash basin, and returned to the stranger on the floor. She laid the cloth against his cheek and his brow. He slowly opened his eyes. Instinctively she stood and backed up a few steps.

Blaine found he was still in the second suite, but clearly in the past. A woman, Penelope Burke, was leaning over him as he lay on the floor just inside the door. As his eyes focused, he saw her stand quickly and step back cautiously. She was clearly dressed in a nightgown, apparently preparing to retire for the evening. Her chestnut hair hung in soft waves nearly to her waist. Her face was delicate with what many call 'doe eyes', round and dark. Her skin was velvety soft, untouched by make-up, allowing her natural beauty to show.

"Don't be afraid," Blaine spoke, "I won't hurt you. You must be Penelope Burke," he concluded, getting to his feet, but remaining in place.

"You have me at a disadvantage, Sir. What is your name?"

"Blaine. Blaine Duncan."

"To my knowledge, Sir, this is your third visit to Burkeshire Manor. How is it that we may finally speak?"

Blaine rubbed his head and said, as much to himself as to her, "I'm still trying to figure that one out."

"You realize, of course, that it is most unseemly to have a male visitor in my private chamber."

"Yes, and I'm sorry about that. It's just that I was following the paintings."

"I beg your pardon. What are you saying?"

Blaine didn't know what to say next. "Look, Miss Burke…"

"Mrs. Burke," she corrected.

"I'm sorry, Mrs. Burke. May I sit down over there?" he asked, pointing to the chair at the easel near the window. He still felt a bit light-headed and didn't want to risk fainting again.

"Yes, of course," she answered. She moved herself to the edge of the bed and sat as well.

As it turned out, Penelope began the conversation. "You see, Mr. Duncan, the first time I saw you, you were standing in the master suite looking down at me as I visited my babies in the cemetery. The second time, I found you, if you will pardon my saying so, weeping at the top of the stairs. I reached out to you then, but you simply vanished. And now I find you in my private chamber. While I do not find you threatening, Mr. Duncan, I do feel an explanation is in order."

Blaine was lost in listening to her. It was incredible. She was clearly a woman of great charm and beauty, but obviously fearless as well. Somehow he had invaded her time and space and yet she was not afraid.

"Mr. Duncan," she repeated. "I'm waiting for an explanation."

"Mrs. Burke. What I have to say may sound a bit strange to you."

"Could it possibly be stranger than a man disappearing before my eyes at the top of my stairs?"

"Well, maybe. You see, they're my stairs, too. What year is this, Mrs. Burke?"

"Why, it's the year of our Lord 1693. What a strange question, Mr. Duncan."

"Is it? Look at me, Mrs. Burke. Look at my clothing. Do I look like I belong here? For you it is 1693, but for me, at least before I came here tonight, the year is 2017 and in that year, this is my house."

Blaine had risen from his chair and he suddenly realized he was in the identical spot he'd seen himself in the painting.

"Why, then, have you come to me?" Penelope asked, undaunted by his explanation.

"I don't know, Ma'am. I don't know. But if the paintings are as accurate as I believe they are, I do know this, I most certainly will be back."

"I don't understand," Penelope began, but she didn't get a chance to finish her question. Without any warning, just as before, he was gone. He simply vanished before her eyes. Her unfinished question was left unspoken.

At this point, the only thing she felt certain of was that she would get little sleep tonight. She felt no fear over the encounter, no anxiety, not even the slightest apprehension. Indeed, she was intrigued, even fascinated. There was a sense of exhilaration and anticipation. She recalled her comments to Chloe of when she felt she was standing at the edge of the great precipice and that her life about to change in ways she couldn't possibly imagine. Tonight's encounter had certainly justified that premonition. And what an encounter this had been! She had touched him and found him to be a living, breathing man. They had been able to converse, though only for a short time. He had a name, Blaine Duncan, and amazingly, he had already known her name, though he did not seem to be aware of her marital status. Nor did he seem to feel strongly one way or the other when he learned she was indeed a Mrs. That would indicate that his travels to her were not motivated by feelings of love for her. In fact, based on his apparent confusion as to how he got there, it likely had nothing to do with his own intent.

Based on all the evidence available to her at this time, Penelope concluded, at least for now, that they were both unwitting participants in events beyond their control. Whether these events were by purpose or chance, she could not be certain. If by purpose, then whose purpose? Mr. Duncan had stated that he was trying to follow the paintings. This statement made no sense to her. Yes, she was an artist and had many paintings, but she failed to see either how he would know about her paintings, or even if hers were the paintings he referring to. There had been insufficient time to inquire of him further before he vanished once again.

"His house." that's what he had said, "in the year 2017." That was more than 300 years from now. Surely this house would not still be here in 300 years. Or would it? It had been constructed in the finest manner, to be sure. Levi had seen to that. But still, that was indeed a long time.

Penelope considered all these details long into the night, unable to gain any further insight. Eventually, she limited her recollections to his parting words, "he would be back." She found a strange comfort in those words though she was not entirely sure why. Nevertheless, it was upon those words wherein she finally found sleep.

I must admit I was sincerely pleased with myself at this moment in time. Their first encounter had gone exceptionally well. Their willingness to conceive of the inconceivable was gratifying. What a pity more mortals were not open to the endless possibilities of time. I realize, of course, that for Blaine Duncan things had not yet reached a point of fascination and wonder as they had for Penelope. He was holding somewhere between apprehension and concerns for his sanity. Nevertheless, I had great faith in his ability to adapt. It was just a matter of time.

Blaine, too, had found sleep elusive that night. He had found himself at one moment trying to explain the unexplainable to a woman who had died a quarter of a century ago, why he was standing in her bedroom, and the next moment found himself in the same room in the present, with unfinished wallpaper hanging where he had left it, and a wall half torn open where he had found and removed that same woman's paintings; which she apparently had not yet made. And while he was certain these events had indeed occurred, he could not think of a single reason why. None of it made any sense.

He lay on his bed looking from one painting to the next. In painting number three he saw himself standing in Penelope Burke's suite where he had been only hours before. It was uncanny, just as it was with the first and second paintings. His eyes rested on painting number four. There he stood in the cemetery, with only three small graves showing. It was spring by the look of the surrounding foliage. Penelope Burke was there as well. For this night's travel through time, he had purposely chosen the clothes he wore to match those in the painting. He had chosen to go in the evening as had been depicted in the painting. This had been a test. But now that he had proven the painting had represented a reality, he felt that perhaps he had a choice. What if he refused to go to the cemetery this spring? Or, what if he refused to wear the clothing he was shown to wear in painting number four? Could he stop this? Could he show that he was not subject to a pre-destined event? Could he change what happened in time by his own will? He wondered. And even if he could, should he? Was there a purpose or reason why these events should take place? There were 33 paintings. If he allowed it, that would mean 30 more trips through time. What could be so important that he traveled more than 300 years 30 more times? What if the number of trips ended at 33 because, for some reason, he had been unable to return the last time? Did he want to risk being trapped over 300 years in the past?

These and a multitude of other questions flooded his mind as the hours dragged on. It was near dawn before he finally slept.

CHAPTER 6

The next morning Blaine decided he needed to get away from the manor for the day. He was afraid he was getting too wrapped up in Penelope's paintings and trying to figure out what was happening and why. About 10 a.m. he called Jack Rush and offered to buy him lunch if he would tell him which place was the best in town for lunch.

"Well, that's got to be Maxine's on the corner of Fifth and Pike. They make a mean burger with all the fixin's. You'd swear you were back in the 50s."

Blaine thought, "I've been a lot further back than that," but he didn't say it. Instead, he said, "Sounds perfect. Meet you there at noon then?"

"Sounds great, see you then."

Jack had been by a few times in the last three months, but Blaine had always declined invitations for bowling or get-togethers with the guys on the force, for a night of poker and beer. Jack had taken the refusals well and always stayed for a short visit anyway, but Blaine knew he was worried about him being alone so much. He thought meeting him for lunch today would set his mind at ease. And Blaine also thought he might do himself some good and set his own mind at rest for a few hours. This business with having traveled back through time had really set his nerves on end. He couldn't dismiss it as though it was nothing, but he also couldn't control it. He felt completely at the mercy of these events and that was a feeling he didn't like at all. What was worse, he couldn't exactly sit down and talk about it with anyone. They would likely lock him up in some mental hospital believing the death of his wife had sent him over the edge. All he could do was get away from the manor for a while and hope he didn't suddenly vanish in front of Jack during lunch.

Winter was definitely coming to an end. There were only a few patches of snow in shaded areas and a week of sunny days would have those gone in no time. April was just a couple of weeks away, and everyone in town seemed to be looking forward to having winter behind them. Before meeting Jack, Blaine stopped at the hardware store to pick up some supplies to repair the wall in the second suite. Gabe Ingram was behind the counter when he brought the items up to check out.

"Looks like we might get an early spring," he said, with a broad, friendly smile. "Myself, I think it's the best time of year. Everything starts new. I always thought April should be the first month of the year, then count out from there. Everything is so dead and cold in January, you know."

Blaine smiled and nodded, but Gabe didn't seem to need him to add anything to the conversation. He was happy to ramble on by himself.

"Bet you'll have that place ship shape and open for business in no time. We're sure glad you stayed. Yes, sir, we've been waiting a long time." Gabe stopped talking suddenly as though he thought he'd said something he shouldn't, then started up again, "Well, here's your change, Mr. Duncan. You have a real good day now, you hear."

"Thanks, Gabe. You, too."

Blaine wondered what that was all about as he loaded his supplies into the truck. He wondered who "we" was and what "we" have been waiting for." Gabe was a good guy, about Jack's age. He'd always been real friendly with Blaine but it always seemed like there was something he wanted to say but didn't. It's like he always decided to say a bunch of useless stuff instead, kind of like today. He put it out of his mind. The last thing he needed was another mystery to solve, even a small one.

Jack's cruiser was already parked in front of Maxine's when Blaine got there. The whole place was done up 50s style inside and out. Blaine joined Jack in the apple-red vinyl booth. The tabletop size jukebox set against the wall between them was filled with all the hits from the 50s and the 60s according to the sign on top. That was a little before Blaine's time, but nostalgia was always fun.

They looked through the menu which hosted a dozen types of burgers, including one called the belly buster. They both made a selection a little more manageable, then settled back to visit while they waited for their order.

"I gotta say," Jack began, "it's good to see you out for a change."

"Yeah, you know how it is. Lots of work to do and just me doin' it."

"Like I said before, there's a lot of folks in town willing to pitch in."

"Actually, I have given that some thought. With spring coming, I could use some people to help get the grounds in shape. I'd pay a fair wage if you know anyone who'd be interested. A little landscaping experience would be good."

"I'll put the word out. It shouldn't take too long to come up with some good men. So, how about you? Have you got a better handle on things yet?"

"You mean have I got a handle on Christina being dead and gone? I don't know, you tell me. Have you got a handle on your wife being dead and gone?" His words came out much harsher than he intended. He hung his head, sighed; then he said, "I'm sorry, Jack, I didn't mean that the way it sounded."

Jack seemed to understand. "You're right, Blaine, I guess you never really get over something like that. In time, it does get easier to manage."

"Still, I'm sorry. I had no right to say it like that. I know you're just being a friend, and I was just acting like a jerk. It's funny, some days I think I've gotten on top of it, and then other days, I'm ready to bite someone's head off. It makes me crazy sometimes."

"I hear you. For what it's worth, I think it's good for you to get out once in a while like this. It reminds you that there's still life out there."

Their burgers arrived and there was little conversation for a while. Blaine was considering inquiring about the house's history but wanted to choose his words carefully.

"So, Jack, been around here long?"

"Second generation. My folks moved here when they got married. My dad was chief of police for thirty years. They moved to Westport when he retired."

"That long? So what can you tell me about the manor?"

"The manor? Well, it's been here since the late 1600s; been completely renovated at least twice, as far as I know."

"Who built it? Do you know anything about that?"

"Guy by the name of Burke. Levi Burke if I recall. He was big in the lumber industry if memory serves. Why? You writing a history or something?"

"No. Just thought having a little history on the place would be good for the paying customers. It was Christina's idea."

"And not a bad one if you ask me. Maybe Lucy at the library can help you. You should stop in and see her sometime."

"I'll do that, thanks." He paused a moment then asked, "Have you ever heard of anything, I don't know, strange about the place?"

Jack chuckled. "What, like ghosts or something?"

"I don't know. Awe, forget it, Christina just thought it would be good for business if the place was, you know, haunted or something."

Jack didn't laugh this time. "Is everything okay up there, Blaine?"

Blaine knew he had said too much. He tried to backpedal. "Yeah, sure. I was just thinking of ideas to bring in the tourists. Gotta think of business you know."

"Right. Well, I'll see what I can do about getting you some able-bodied men for work on the grounds. Shouldn't take more than a couple of days to find the right guys."

"Great. Well, you were right, that was the best burger I've eaten in years. Guess I'll head back home. Got lots of work waiting. I've got this," he said, grabbing the check.

"Alright, buddy, I'll be talking to you soon."

After Blaine left, Jack sat a while in the booth absently running a french-fry through the ketchup on his plate in a repeating pattern. He suspected from Blaine's comment that things had already started. He wished he could tell him now, but he knew it was too soon. He had to wait until the time was right. And he had to make sure that Gabe Ingram kept his mouth shut, too. This whole thing had to unfold naturally. They would just have to be patient.

Before Jack went home for some much needed sleep, he pulled the cruiser up to Ingrahm's Hardware Store and went in for a word with Gabe. Jack waited until there were no customers near the counter that might overhear their conversation.

"Hey, Jack. What's up?"

"I think it's started," Jack said, purposely being vague because of passing customers.

"Why?" Gabe's eyes widened with interest. "What did he tell you?"

"He didn't really say anything specific, but he asked if I had ever heard of anything strange happenings at the manor. Then he tried to cover himself by suggesting a good ghost story would be good for business with the guests. It's not much, but I definitely got the sense that something has happened."

Jack expected Gabe to be a little excited at this news, but instead, Gabe looked down at the counter in uncharacteristic silence. Finally, he spoke. "Ever since we were kids I've been anxiously waiting to see if things would happen the way the book said. Then, when Duncan actually showed up in Machias and bought the manor, well, it was a wow moment and kinda thrilling. But now..."

"What are you trying to say, Gabe?"

"I don't know. I guess I'm just saying that, at first it was all kind of exciting. But now, if things are actually starting to happen, I mean, it's kinda creepin' me out. Maybe we shouldn't get any deeper into this."

They both stopped talking for a minute when Nancy Keller came up to the counter carrying two gallons of paint and some other painting supplies.

"How ya doing, Nancy?" Gabe said. "Looks like you finally talked Tom into paining that fence."

"Finally," she nodded, smiling.

They chatted a few minutes while Jack pretended to be looking at some drain cleaner. When she left, Jack went back to Gabe.

"If this creeps you out, you know you don't have to be involved, but I don't have a choice. It's already done. How do you stop something that's already done?"

Gabe nodded his understanding. Both had made their decisions. They shook hands without further comment.

"Be careful," Gabe said as Jack walked out of the store.

MARCH 13, 1693

Penelope had given considerable thought to her brief visit with Mr. Duncan; in particular, to his comment about following the paintings. It occurred to her that her entire life would have passed long before he took possession of the home in the future. Therefore, she must have made some kind of effort to guide him to her at some point. Perhaps that effort had been the paintings he was referring to. And, she thought she must have put them somewhere where they could be discovered by him.

She browsed through the many painting she had already made, hoping something would stand out to her. One did. It was the view of the house from the cemetery where she had seen him for the first time in the window of the master suite. Neither he nor she was currently in the painting. She set the finished painting on the easel once again and began to add first him in the window, and then herself in the foreground, looking up. Perhaps this would become the guiding factor he had been referring to. She decided she would create a painting for each time they met in hopes they would find their way into his hands one day.

As she worked at the easel that day, she began to marvel at the fluid nature of time. Creating this map, as it were, in art form was an idea he had given her by his comment. Yet he would not have made such a comment had she not, at some point, made these paintings for him to follow. How wonderfully odd and fantastic this was—a mystery in the making. One that, perhaps, they would never solve; for to solve it would change its very nature. For the first time since she had come to Burkeshire Manor, Penelope Burke found herself looking forward with eager anticipation for what was to come.

Blaine Duncan, on the other hand, had not seen the beauty of it. In fact, he felt some resentment that he had been distracted from his personal misery by these paintings and ensuing travel through time. He further resented the implication by these paintings that he had no say in the matter. He had always believed he was the master of his own destiny and for better or worse, he alone would determine his fate. Yet, the paintings indicated otherwise.

Today he had nearly made himself look foolish when talking to Jack about ghost stories. He slammed his hand against the steering wheel in frustration as he turned the truck toward home. He would not stop at the library today or any other day. He would go home and continue working to make Christina's dreams come true. He would keep his promise to her, no matter how lonely and difficult it was without her. He would gather up the paintings and put them away somewhere where he wouldn't have to look at them. He would forget about Penelope Whittier Burke and think only of Christina and the promise he had made. And he would start right now!

As he drove, he felt the anger and frustration growing in him. He didn't try to push it away. Instead, he savored it. He let it build until it consumed him, giving him the strength he needed to defy fate and live on his own terms. "I'm in control of my life," he declared aloud to the invisible powers around him. "I'll decide what I will and won't do." His voice was loud and fierce. More fierce than he had ever heard himself, but he was determined to not let go of the fierceness. And even though, somewhere deep inside he knew this was wrong, he was determined to hold onto it, for it would carry him through. For now, he needed that more than anything.

For the next forty-five days or so Blaine worked unceasingly to keep his promise. He hired two men to begin restoring the grounds. He also hired Becky McCutchen from the antique shop to assist him in designing the remaining rooms, ordering wallpaper, rugs, fixtures and other such items to complement the new furnishings. Jack came by a couple of times with Dan Starkey, from the force, to help him get the heavy furnishings upstairs and into the appropriate rooms. In a month and a half, the second suite and the third bedroom on the second floor were done. He even updated the bathroom on that floor with new paint, a replica claw foot tub with an adjustable shower head hung from an ornate brass work overhead, and appropriate linen. He had left the floors in the corridor until last so as not to add damage while moving heavy furniture.

Through it all, Blaine remained focused. He was cordial with Becky, Jack and the others, but avoided small talk and especially any discussion of how he was doing personally. He was all business and was determined to keep it that way. If he didn't, if he let even the smallest emotion in, his house of cards would crumble. He didn't even allow himself time to visit with Christina throughout this period of work, though he did think of her each night as he lay in bed. That was the only time he allowed himself to do so.

It was one such night in late April when he laid thinking of Christina that something came to him that he had forgotten since the day of the accident. He was thinking of the last time she spoke to him, and how she had reminded him of his promise to her. But, there had been more. At the time, he thought she was confused because what she had said made no sense to him. Now he thought of the words again. "She will help you." What had Christina been trying to tell him? Was she talking about Penelope Burke? He thought how he had heard stories of people who were near death suddenly being aware of things. Things they couldn't possibly know, but somehow did, as though they had a tenuous grasp on a world beyond this one. In those moments before she died, had Christina somehow been aware of or even communicated with Penelope?

And, if so, was she telling him to let her help him? Help him do what, he wondered. He thought of how driven he had been these past weeks. He had denied his own feelings for fear they would devour his newfound strength, a strength built on anger and frustration. He began to recognize that he had become a different man. Not the man he had been with Christina. Maybe Christina saw this coming. Maybe she was afraid he would harden his heart to avoid the pain. Maybe she thought Penelope Burke could somehow help him to deal with all this. He didn't know. There had not been time for explanations before she died. But he did know this, if he was to ever know peace, he would need to give in to the possibility that Christina was right.

"She can help you." He wouldn't know for sure unless he allowed himself to go back at least one more time.

CHAPTER 7

Blaine awoke the next morning to sun streaming in the windows of his room. It was Sunday morning. No one would be coming today; the groundskeepers, Mrs. McCutchen, they would not be here. No one here in this sleepy little town seemed to work on Sundays. Blaine would have the place to himself. As it turned out, he was fine with that; he had his own plans for the day.

He made himself a light breakfast and ate before walking out to the workshop. Most of the furniture he had been working on was now finished and had been brought into the house for placement in its appropriate room. The only remaining pieces were two side tables waiting to be made ready for the second floor corridor and a very large trunk, pushed to the back of the work room. He went to the trunk and lifted the lid, bracing it with some scrap wood. Inside, a quilted moving blanket covered its contents. He folded back the blanket to reveal the 33 paintings he had packed away defiantly in March. He thumbed through the paintings until he came to painting number four. He carefully slipped it out of the collection, drew the blanket over the remaining paintings, and closed the trunk. He carried the painting back to the house and settled himself in the kitchen to examine it again.

He first took in the background. It was clearly a spring day as it was today. The setting was the cemetery. Of course, only three graves existed in this portrayal. And then, there was Penelope Burke together with Blaine, apparently conversing. He wondered what they had been talking about, or, perhaps, what they would soon be talking about. Finally, he observed the specific clothing he was wearing in the painting. Strangely, it was the very same clothing he had chosen to wear this morning. A brief shiver ran up his spine. "If I was looking for confirmation, this is it," he thought. He glanced up at the clock on the wall. It read 10:55 a.m.

Now was as good a time as any. Blaine left the painting lying on the kitchen table, then stepped out the kitchen door and made his way to the cemetery. Once there, he walked to Christina's grave first. He still had not ordered a headstone for her grave. He couldn't bring himself to take, what he considered to be, that final step. Nevertheless, there was no mistaking the specific location. The entire ground had been covered with snow these past months and only recently been exposed to spring warmth and the very beginnings of new spring growth.

He stood quietly for a moment, ordering his thoughts. Even so, he was somewhat surprised at the first words out of his mouth. "I'm sorry honey. I know I haven't been to see you for a while. I guess I just didn't want you to see me while I was so, well, not myself. I know I've been kind of hard. I just haven't quite known how to be here without you. But last night I was thinking about something you told me before. Well, I don't know if you know what's been going on here, but I'm guessing you do. Or, at least, you knew what was coming before you left." He knew he was rambling. "Anyway, I thought maybe somehow you knew this was all going to happen. Maybe you knew I was going to be traveling through time. I can't believe I'm even saying this—it still sounds so crazy. Maybe you thought Penelope Burke could help me, I don't know, deal with you being gone. Anyway, I guess we'll see what happens."

At this point he had finished his oration. He fully expected to be suddenly transported through time, but nothing happened. He had been standing with his back to the bulk of the cemetery facing Christina's grave at the outermost edge of the cemetery grounds. He turned to face the other graves, half expecting all but three of them to be gone and Penelope Burke standing there. Still, nothing changed. He turned his palms up with his arms outstretched as though he were surrendering himself to the inevitable. Again, nothing changed. "Well, for crying out loud!" he said. "What do you want me to do?" he called out to no one in particular. Still, nothing changed.

"Forget this," he said, making a rude gesture to the sky. "You've had your chance. I'm outta here."

He turned quickly in the direction of the house, but maybe a bit too quickly. He stopped suddenly, holding his head, waiting for the moment of dizziness to pass. Then he heard her.

"It would be ever so much more convenient, Mr. Duncan, if you could somehow forewarn me of your impending visits."

Blaine raised his head to see Penelope Burke standing about ten feet away, near the graves of her children. Her voice held a hint of amusement and there was a smile on her face, indicating she was pleased to see him.

Blaine smiled back. "I would if I could. I've only been able to figure out the where, but not the when."

"I see. Shall I conclude then that you had other cause to be in the cemetery this day, and our visit is by chance?"

"I was visiting my wife," he said, gesturing behind him to where Christina's grave should be.

Penelope understood. "I, too, have come to see my loved ones past. May I present my darling babies, now angels." She stretched out her hand toward the three small graves of her children.

"I'm sorry," Blaine offered. "All of them?"

"They are three of seven. Four of my children reside with me in the manor."

Blaine nodded his understanding.

Penelope asked, "May I inquire of your wife?"

"Sure. Umm, she died about four months ago in a car accident."

"I'm sorry for your loss, Mr. Duncan. Forgive me, but I must ask, what is a car?"

"A car?" It hadn't occurred to him she would have no way of knowing what that was. "Well a car is something like a carriage, only without the horses. Instead, it has a fuel combustion engine which gives it the power to move much faster than a carriage."

"I'm sorry, Mr. Duncan, I'm afraid I'm not as learned as you apparently are."

Blaine jumped in. "Oh, no, no, no, I'm sorry, I didn't mean to make you feel, well, I mean, it has been 300 years. Some things have changed, is all."

"Yes, of course. I am truly sorry for the death of your wife in the car."

"Thank you, Mrs. Burke. I appreciate that. You are certainly someone who understands. I was actually talking to her about you today. Well, what I mean is, she said something to me before she died that I have only recently remembered. As strange as it sounds, I think she was talking about you."

"I find some comfort in knowing you speak with your wife as I do to my darling Angels. I sometimes question if I am not completely rational in doing so."

Blaine looked beyond the cliffs of the cemetery to the ocean waters. "I'm not sure I could handle it if I didn't think I could talk to her once in a while. I don't think there's any reason to question if that's rational."

Penelope laughed softly and said, "I have just been reassured of my sanity by a man who will not be born for 300 years."

Blaine smiled at the irony.

"Nevertheless, I am grateful for your assurances."

They had fallen into step together and begun moving along the top of the cliffs overlooking the ocean.

"Tell me, Mr. Duncan, what did your wife say to you before she died?"

"Before I tell you about that," he said, "I'd like to talk to you about the paintings you made, or rather, will make. I found them in the second suite wall. I guess that would be in what is now your room. You made a painting for each time I travel back here. You signed them and numbered them. Today is painting number four."

"That's incredible! I suspected as much after our last visit. You mentioned at that time that you were following the paintings. I speculated about such a possibility. How many paintings are there, Mr. Duncan?"

"There are thirty-three. I assume that means I will have at least thirty-three visits here."

Penelope was encouraged. She had wondered if there would be time to develop a friendship. She desperately needed a friend, although she would never say so to Mr. Duncan. She only said, "It's a bit like cheating, don't you think? No one should know the future, and yet we do. At least, a bit of it. That is, of course, if the paintings are correct."

"They have been so far." He paused a moment, then said, "Don't you feel a little like—I don't know—like a puppet? I mean it seems like someone, something else is calling the shots. Things like when I come, where I come, how long I stay, and so on. Do you know what I mean?"

"I hadn't considered that perspective," she admitted. "I must say I have found it somewhat exhilarating. But then, I am not the one who is traveling. It is you who is apparently being pulled from one reality to another at random moments. I suppose that would tend to make one feel out of control. For my part, I have enjoyed your company, Mr. Duncan. It has been rare when I have had the opportunity to speak to someone outside the residents of the manor. As bizarre as this experience has thus far been, it has been a welcome variation in my sadly predictable life."

"I'm afraid my life is anything but predictable, especially now. Christina and I had everything planned. But now, she's gone and I'm jumping back and forth through time without warning. I don't even know why it's happening or how to stop or even control it. Personally, I would be grateful for a little predictability."

"I am sorry, Mr. Duncan, but you are not facing this alone. I am willing to offer whatever insight or support I am can. And, I'm guessing your wife had some counsel as well. So, may I inquire once again, what did your wife say before she died?"

Blaine stopped walking and looked at Penelope. He had found a level of companionship with her thus far, and perhaps they both needed that. "She said, 'she can help you.' I think she was talking about you."

"How fascinating!" Penelope said. "Did she explain?"

"I'm afraid not. She was very close to death and was barely able to speak. At the time, I thought she was confused. Her words make no sense to me. We were quite new to the community and there was simply no "she" I could imagine Christina could have been referring to. Then, this began to happen. She could only have been referring to you."

Penelope said nothing for a moment. She seemed to be uncomfortable. Finally, she responded, "I'm afraid my view of the situation has been somewhat different. You see, Mr. Duncan, I must confess, I have been looking to you as the one who could help me."

Blaine did not yet see what sort of help could be to her. Admittedly he had little insight into her life as of yet, but her life seemed far more in control than his at the moment. He was not sure how he should respond to her comment. He needn't have been concerned. He suddenly found himself on the cliffs a short distance from the cemetery—his cemetery, alone. Apparently whoever or whatever was controlling his travels through time had decided it was time to come home.

Jack Rush had been concerned about Blaine the last several weeks. His easy-going manner had changed and he had thrown himself into the renovation of the manor. He had become distant. Jack knew he was mourning Christina. He had done the same when his wife had passed. He had avoided social contact and taken extra shifts at work. But, he thought, Blaine must not be me. Blaine had a purpose waiting for him, even if he didn't know it. Jack had to gain his trust and guide him. He couldn't let him shut out his heart and just go through the motions of life. Jack felt it was his responsibility to be there for Blaine whether Blaine wanted him to or not. Besides, Jack liked him. He could see that Blaine was a good man. Jack had waited most of his life for Blaine Duncan. Many of those years he questioned whether he was even real. Except for Gabe Ingram, no one else knew about this, and the two of them had only been boys, ages twelve and thirteen, when they'd found it. Though they knew it was important, they had still been too young to appreciate its full value. Jack, being the oldest of the two, (though only by eight months), declared himself to be the keeper of the treasure by virtue of age. Through the years they had kept the secret, even from their wives, and with years of maturity came an even greater sense of awe and wonder at what they had found. But, it wasn't until Blaine Duncan actually came to Machias and purchased the manor that they knew for sure.

Jack decided he would drive out to the manor to check on Blaine. He knew there would be no one working there today and maybe he could have a good visit with him. With any luck, he could find out a few things. He glanced at the clock before heading out to his truck. It read 10:30 a.m. It would only take him about ten or fifteen minutes to get there.

He pulled up to the house and walked around to the kitchen entrance. He knocked, but couldn't see Blaine through the window in the door. He knocked again, pushing the door open and called for Blaine. He didn't see or hear him.

"Blaine, it's Jack. Are you in here?" Still no answer. Jack was about to close the door and look for him outside when something caught his eye. It was the painting Blaine had left on the kitchen table. Jack left the door open and went to the table for a closer look. He was stunned. The painting was old. It was a depiction of the old cemetery of Burkeshire Manor with a woman from that time in the foreground. She was clearly speaking with the man who was also in the cemetery: Blaine Duncan. It didn't take his police training to know it was indeed Blaine. He didn't just look like Blaine. His clothing and hair were not typical of the period. He knew it was Blaine, and he knew the woman was Penelope Whittier Burke.

"Damn!" Blaine shouted. "Whoever you are that's doing this, you could at least give us a little more time to figure this out. Who put you in charge anyway!"

I must admit I was a bit wounded by that outburst. After all, I was sincerely working with their best interests at heart. You would think one would be a little more appreciative. Whether he understood or not, I had my reasons for keeping their visits brief for now. They both needed time to absorb their new reality in small doses. Otherwise, they both would start breaking off into useless obsessions on *how* and completely overlook the *why*. The *why* was all that mattered. Penelope had begun to focus on the *why* already. Blaine, however, was still tied up in the *how*. I consider myself to be of considerable patience. When one's work involves managing all of time, that is clearly a prerequisite. However, Blaine Duncan was beginning to try my patience. That is why I decided to let Jack Rush give me a little help.

I reached back into the year 1983 and found Jack Rush and his friend Gabe Ingram sneaking through a broken window on the main floor of the manor. The place was going through another period of vacancy and it had been empty for about seven years, as I recall. Jack was thirteen and Gabe twelve. The two had been best friends since they started school. In August of this year they had decided to do something adventuresome this one last time before the new school year began. Childhood tales of the place being haunted, (Isn't every old empty house haunted?), had prompted them to spend the night there as a show of bravery. Of course their parents believed each was spending the night at the other's house. Each of the boys had filled their backpacks with all the essential gear necessary for the investigation of ghosts. Things like chocolate bars, soda, chips, flashlights, and even some dried garlic. You never know when you might run into a vampire.

I'm not generally fond of exposing the end before the beginning, but in this case, I felt Jack could give Blaine the push he needed when the time came, so on that night in 1983, I handed Jack the end, believing he would know when to use it. It was that night when Jack's foot crunched through a rotting floorboard, exposing a square metal container. Lifting it out and carefully opening the box, he found the journal inside. Gabe came running from the next room to see the treasure he had found. They could see the dates beginning in 1695 and going until 1725. A final entry was made in 1755. It was the content that made their find a treasure and made them determined to keep the secret. It made several references to a woman by the name of Penelope Burke and her friend and eventually her love, Blaine Duncan. It told of a man who had come to her from the future and brought happiness to her life and his. It explained how they had met by sharing the same space in different times and somehow had the experience of those times being brought together. Essentially, time travel. The boys determined that within their lifetime, in approximately thirty-two years, the details of this record could be either proven or disproven.

First, a man by the name of Blaine Michael Duncan would need to take possession of the manor. Later the paintings would need to be found. That would be something the boys couldn't do because the record indicated that Blaine would find them himself. There had been nothing more for the boys to do but keep the secret and wait. When Blaine had shown up in August, 2016, and taken possession of the manor on September first, Jack's wait had come to an end. He and Gabe were watching a prophecy fulfilled; the present preparing to touch the past. Waiting for the right moment to reveal this journal to Blaine would probably be even more difficult than waiting for his arrival these past thirty-two years.

CHAPTER 8

As Blaine made his way back from his cemetery, he was surprised to see Jack Rush standing there waiting for him with something in his hand. Blaine was still trying to pull himself together from the jump through time, and was not sure he was up to talking to Jack at this point. As he got closer, he could see that Jack had something serious on his mind and that caused Blaine to look more closely at what he held in his hand. It was the painting. The one he'd left on the kitchen table. Blaine's mind quickly began to work, trying to come up with an explanation for the painting. He needn't have bothered. Jack spoke first. It wasn't what Jack said that confused Blaine, but the fact that he had seemed casual, not at all surprised when he said it. That put Blaine at ease, somewhat, but he was still confused.

"I see you've been to see her," Jack said, lifting the painting to view. "It's alright, Blaine, I've just been waiting for the right time to talk to you about this. So… shall we go inside?"

Blaine was completely speechless. He had been guarding the secret so closely, but now it seemed that Jack had known all along. How could he, and why did he seem so happy to finally be able to talk about it? Finally he found his voice. "You knew? Why didn't you say something?"

"The same reason you never said anything to me. You were afraid I would think you were crazy, and I was afraid you would think the same of me if I told you first. So, got any more of that Jack Daniels left?"

"I'm sure I could find something that would suffice."

They returned to the house together and Jack took his usual seat at the kitchen table while Blaine grabbed a couple of beers out of the fridge, handing one to Jack and sitting down across from him with the painting on the table between them.

"Do you know about all of them?" Blaine asked, "The paintings, I mean."

"All I knew was that there were paintings. I never knew how many, or what was in them."

"But how could you know? They were in the wall. I only found them by accident a couple of months ago. If you knew about them, then there must be something else you're not telling me."

"There is more, Blaine. If I had known we were going to be talking about this today, I would have brought it with me. The story actually started a long time ago, when I was thirteen. The manor was empty then, and most of the kids in town thought it was haunted. Gabe Ingram and I decided to check it out one night, and that's when we found the journal."

"I don't get it. What journal?"

"When Gabe and I were just kids, we found a journal hidden in a metal box under the floor here in the manor. We started reading it and discovered that it was talking about time travel. The journal had been written by Penelope Burke and it was about her and the man that came to her through time from the future. She named the man. It was you, Blaine—Blaine Michael Duncan. The journal talked about all the visits that they would have together over the years and about the relationship that developed between them. Of course, we had no way of knowing if it was real or true, because you had not come to town yet, and wouldn't for another thirty-two years. Only then, would we know if the things that were written were true and if you were a real person and were indeed going to travel back in time to visit Penelope Burke. Gabe and I made a promise that day that we would never tell anyone, but wait and see if you would ever show up. You can imagine how excited we were when we learned last year that Blaine Michael Duncan and his wife had just purchased the manor."

Blaine listened in astonishment as Jack explained what he and Gabe Ingram had uncovered and how they had kept the secret and waited with anxious anticipation all these years. Jack was clearly excited to be able to finally share this extraordinary news with Blaine, but Blaine did not share his excitement.

That old feeling that his life was not under his own control was back. From what Jack was telling him, his entire future—years of time—was already written. Every decision, every action, already taken and just waiting to be played out. He couldn't accept that. He was in control of his life. He had to believe that. If that were not true, then what purpose was there? Why strive to improve one's self? Why exercise self-discipline? Why make any choices at all?

"No." Blaine said, getting to his feet and beginning to pace back and forth in the kitchen. "I can't accept that, Jack. This isn't right. People's lives are not pre-ordained. We make our own choices. Don't you believe that?"

"Yes, I do, but then how do you explain the journal, and these paintings? Let me run home and get the journal. You can see for yourself."

"No. I don't want to see it. I don't want to be influenced in any way."

Blaine almost sounded angry. Jack was confused. "Well, if you don't want to see the journal, can I see the other paintings? I mean, you've already seen them, so it's not like we're introducing anything new to you."

Blaine tried to calm that old familiar frustration at the way his life seemed to be spinning out of control since Christina died. "Look, Jack. I can see you're excited about all this and maybe I would be, too, if I had waited for this moment as many years as you have, but try to look at it from my point of view. I feel like I've just discovered I'm a side show attraction for some cosmic circus owner and my life is on display. It makes me feel like I'm part of a pre-written script. That's not a good feeling, Jack. Can you understand that?"

Jack had to admit that he could. Up until this moment, he had never looked at it from Blaine's point of view. Nevertheless, his desire to see the paintings remained.

Blaine could see Jack was trying to understand. He had to admit to himself that Jack had been a good friend through all this and he was grateful. And the fact that Jack's revelation meant he did not have to deal with this spontaneous time travel alone was a degree of comfort. He curbed his anxiety enough to say, "You're right, Jack. I've already seen the paintings. What would it hurt if you saw them, too? Who else can I talk to about this? It does help to have someone to share this with. One condition, though. I know Gabe already knows about the journal, but let's keep the paintings between us. Deal?"

"Deal."

"Okay, they're in the shop. Let's go."

Blaine removed the paintings one by one, leaning them against the wall in the shop. He pointed out the signature and the numbers on each painting, explaining that the trips through time had thus far occurred in the recorded order.

"So, do you know in advance when these trips through time are going to happen?" Jack asked.

"Not really. I only know where from what the picture shows, and I get a sense of when by whether or not there is daylight or dark in the picture and the clothes that I'm wearing. You see here, in today's painting, that I am wearing the same clothes I'm wearing now."

"I wonder why she didn't just put the dates on each painting."

"I don't know. Maybe she thought since we were in different times, the dates wouldn't matter."

Jack looked again at the painting showing today's trip. "So, before I saw you in the cemetery today, you were actually back in time talking with Penelope Burke?"

"Yeah. Crazy, huh?"

"Well, what did you talk about?"

"Not much. We never get much time. Today we were just talking about how strange this is, a little about three of her children that died, and some about Christina."

"How do you know when to come back?"

"I don't. It just happens. Just like when I go. I don't seem to have anything to say about it."

"And she's not...afraid of what's happening?"

"That's the funny thing. She actually seemed glad to see me today, like she'd been waiting for me. I think she's kinda lonely. She's young, about my age, but she seems...strong, or mature for her age. I haven't had the time to really get to know her yet."

Jack looked at the other pictures with Penelope in them. "She's certainly attractive. Does she really look like this?"

"Oh, for Pete's sake, Jack. Christina's barely gone. Do you really think I could be attracted to someone else? Especially someone who's been dead for over 200 years?"

"I didn't mean anything." Jack tried to backpedal by

changing the subject. "So, if today was painting number four, this must be the next time you'll see her." He pointed to painting number five.

It was an interior picture of the manor in what appeared to be the library. No windows were showing in the painting so one could not be sure if it was day or night. Penelope was seated at the piano with her back to the foreground. Blaine stood just inside the entry looking at her.

"Have you seen anyone else besides Penelope on these trips?"

"Not yet, but today I was a bit concerned that someone in the house might look out a window and see us. I'm pretty sure that's why she walked us out on the cliffs. She probably couldn't explain my being there any easier than I could explain disappearing from here. It's maddening not knowing how and why this is happening. Is there some kind of time warp running through this property or what? I don't think I can come to terms with the idea that some intelligence of some kind has a hand in this. I just don't know what to believe. It's crazy."

"Look, Buddy. You should probably bring these in the house. The dampness out here can't be good for them. I'll help."

"Yeah, you're right. I did have them in the house, but I spent too much time looking at them and trying to figure this out. That's why I brought them out here."

"Well, if you want, you can put them away in the house and not look at them, but they shouldn't be out here. Come on, it'll only take a few trips each."

Together, they made several trips into the house, depositing the paintings in the library on the main floor. Jack said he needed to get back to town but promised to keep their secret about the paintings.

"Hang in there, Blaine. Things will sort themselves out." It was a flimsy bit of encouragement, Jack knew, but it was all he could think to say.

Jack wasn't home more than ten minutes before he had the journal out and began reading again. It had been almost a year since he had looked at it, but there were parts he wanted to review. He hadn't told Blaine that not all his trips to the past were smooth sailing. Jack's intent had been to warn Blaine of some rocky roads ahead, but Blaine had made it clear he didn't want to know what was coming. Jack had to admit he understood, but he was concerned for Blaine just the same. Blaine was no longer just the embodiment of a prophecy fulfilled, he was Jack's friend, and friends don't just stand by when there's trouble coming.

CHAPTER 9

Penelope sat in her room feeling frustrated over the brief visit she'd had today with Mr. Duncan. Although they had learned a bit more about one another, there was so much more she wanted to understand. Judging by previous visits, it would likely be months before they would meet again. It was true that each visit seemed to be longer than the previous one, and she hoped that would continue to be the case. Meanwhile she found herself dreading the weeks to come until his next visit.

As she sat at her easel, hands in her lap, staring out at the cemetery, there was a soft rap at her door.

"Enter," she said distractedly.

The door opened and Chloe stepped in, quietly closing the door behind her.

"Am I disturbing you, Ma'am?" she asked timidly.

"No, Chloe. What is it?"

"Begging your pardon, Ma'am. I...," she stammered, not knowing how to continue.

Penelope could see she was terribly uncomfortable.

"What is it, Chloe? Are the children alright?"

"Oh, yes, Ma'am. The children are fine. I just wondered... this morning I was looking for you and...," She was lost for words again.

Penelope rose from her chair and came to Chloe, placing her hands on Chloe's shoulders.

"My dear Chloe, you're trembling. What is it you are trying to say?"

"Well, Ma'am, I'm sorry. I didn't mean to spy on you. It's just that, well, I went to the cemetery to find you and I saw...a young gentleman there with you. Forgive me, Ma'am. I didn't mean to intrude."

Penelope dropped her hands from Chloe's shoulders and turned away, holding her composure.

"I see," she said quietly. Her mind raced. What would she say now? Could she trust Chloe with this extraordinary secret? Did she really have any choice at this point? She turned back to Chloe, setting a warm smile on her face, and said, "Chloe, you have been my only friend these many years. I would like to share an extraordinary secret with you. May I do that with the assurance it will remain a secret?"

Chloe look apprehensive, but she nodded in affirmation.

Penelope took her hand and led her to a small settee. They sat down together. Penelope turned to her and began. "Do you remember some months ago when I asked you if you had ever felt you were at the edge of a great precipice and that life was about to change?"

Chloe nodded.

"It was true, Chloe. Something strange and wonderful began shortly after that night and has continued on since. You may find what I am about to tell you is difficult to believe. I barely believe it myself. Yet it is true."

Penelope explained her first glimpse of Mr. Duncan from the cemetery as he stood in the window of the master suite and each visit afterward until today. She shared both Blaine's and her perspectives on what was occurring. She explained the loss of his wife, his future ownership of the manor, and all that she could recall of their visits. She discussed the paintings and how they had made their way to Mr. Duncan in the future. When she had finished her unbelievable tale, she sat looking at Chloe, waiting for her response.

Chloe's eyes had grown wider with each detail. Being of Irish decent, Chloe had a naturally pale complexion, bright blue eyes and soft red hair that would curl wildly if not for the fact she gathered it back into a bun at the base of her neck. Her wide eyes did not surprise Penelope, but she was not at all prepared for her response.

Chloe made the sign of the cross and whispered, "I fear this is the work of the devil, Ma'am. What you are telling me cannot be the work of God. I urge you to reject this aberration and speak of it no more. Certainly not to the staff or to Mr. Burke."

"Oh, no, Chloe, you don't understand. Mr. Duncan is a kind man. There is no evil here. Indeed, it is a miracle. He has asked nothing of me and is, indeed, as perplexed at this happening as I. I'm certain there is no ill intent in his heart. Besides, I have no more ability to stop this than I did to begin. Furthermore, I wouldn't if I could. Chloe, you know better than anyone how lonely I have been. Mr. Duncan has brought me a companionship I had come to believe I would never enjoy. Surely there is no evil in that."

Given the intimate nature of their conversation, Chloe pushed past the boundaries of her station to say, "Miss Penelope, you are very dear to me as well; a sister, in many ways. I have mourned the loneliness you have felt these many years. You have borne it with dignity and without complaint. I admire your gentleness and grace. And, yes, I have wished for you the happiness you deserve. But, I beg of you, be cautious. There are events at play here that are not of man. I will keep this secret, in the hope it brings you joy. However, I urge you to take care."

Penelope let go a sigh of relief and embraced Chloe. "Thank you my dear friend. I knew I could trust you."

"You must tell me when he returns," Chloe insisted. "I can't watch over you without knowing what's happening."

"Indeed, I will. It will be our secret."

In March 1693, Levi Burke arrived late one evening in the town of Salem to meet Mr. Lance Buckman to negotiate timber acquisitions for a new mill. The pub in which they would meet was alive with anxious chatter by thirty or more men of the town. Wading through the crowd to his table, Levi overheard the subject of the chatter.

"Hang her," one man declared.

"Hanging a witch does no good. She must be burned alive," another cried.

"What proof is there she is a witch," yet another appealed. "Shall she die without proof?"

The next comments were lost in a sea of voices and angry cries. Levi joined Mr. Buckman at the table.

"What, in God's name, is this about? What is this talk of witches and burning?"

"My apologies, Mr. Burke. A local woman, Mary Hull, was imprisoned this morning on charges of witchcraft. Her husband and children fell suddenly ill with all manner of convulsions and delusional speaking. Mrs. Hull suffered no such illness. It was well known that there was disharmony in the home. Some believe she cast a spell of a devilish nature to rid herself of her husband and children."

"God preserve us," Levi replied. Would a woman sell her soul to the devil for such a purpose?"

"I'm afraid this is not the first," Mr. Buckman said. "Since early last year I, myself, have witnessed the burning of three similarly lost souls. There can be no allowance made for daughters of the devil. We are a God-fearing people. It is our duty to preserve the purity of our homes.

"I have never found that God could do for me what I could

not do for myself. I would wager I am equally independent of the devil's will. Still, I've no wish to test the strength of those words should the need arise. Now, shall we get to the business of your 400 acres of timber?"

Levi spent the next hour with Mr. Buckman, arranging the details and purchase price of their pending business venture. The talk of witchcraft and its consequences boiled over around them, getting more vile as the liquor fueled the men in the pub that night.

Upon retiring to his room in the local boarding house that evening, Levi reflected on the words of the angry, and he thought, frightened men in the pub. He was grateful his family was safely tucked away from such vileness. He was certain his decision to keep them secluded from the flurry of trial and error in building a new world in this vast new land was an act of kindness. He hoped they understood and appreciated his concern for their well-being. He knew his young wife was often lonely, but he believed with some years of maturity she would come to recognize that his protection of seclusion was in her best interest. And on that thought he slept with a clear conscience.

The following morning Levi Burke, business concluded, climbed into his carriage looking once more at the town of Salem as his driver made their way out of the town. At the edge of town Levi saw a great crowd had gathered with cries of "burn the witch" and other obscenities he preferred not to remember. In the midst of the crowd, a woman, presumably Mary Hull, was lifted up upon a large post, held by many lashings of rope. Beneath her feet lay bundles of dry wood soaked in oil. Levi watched in horror as the bundles were lit by a man with a torch. Turning his eyes away, he left Salem to the sound of Mary Hull's screams of pain and the vile shouts of those who were her assassins. Only two short months later, the Salem witch trials would come to an end.

CHAPTER 10

In spite of Blaine's forceful declarations that he did not want to be influenced by signs of the future, he decided to rehang the paintings in the master suite. He told himself it was because he didn't want any of the grounds people or Mrs. McCutchen to stumble across them in the library. As much as he tried to avoid looking at them when he retired to his room each night, he couldn't escape. The next visit recorded was as Jack had described in the library. Some of the following visits included the cliffs, more in the cemetery and yet another in Penelope's suite. Still another was near the carriage house and in a heavily treed area near to it.

Blaine's eyes moved from one painting to another. His thoughts went back and forth between refusal to believe his life was foreordained, and helpless resignation that it had seemed so thus far. It was difficult at best to focus on the task at hand of completing the interior of the manor and preparing the house and grounds as he and Christina had planned. He so wanted to keep his promise to her, yet he had to consider that it may, after all, be out of his hands. That night he drifted off into a fitful sleep, his conflicted emotions conjuring one unsettling dream after another.

Chloe also slept fitfully, and only after lying in her bed for many hours in the small room near the children. She replayed her conversation with Penelope many times, hoping to acquire a peace with these extraordinary events as Penelope obviously had. Yet, try as she might, she could not dispel the fear she felt for her mistress. In spite of her station in this home, she truly loved Penelope as a sister. She felt charged with her safety and well-being, and happily so. She knew that no step to protect her would be too much to ask. Yet, at the same time, she felt helpless to do so. As Penelope had told it, this Mr. Duncan could appear anytime, anywhere. The best Chloe could do was make every attempt to be at Penelope's side as often as possible. What else could she do?

Although previous visits had come months apart, it was only three weeks when Blaine found himself suddenly standing near the door in Penelope Burke's library. Penelope was seated ahead of him at the piano playing a beautiful, but sad piece he did not recognize. She stopped suddenly as she saw him there.

"Mr. Duncan. I was not expecting you." she said.

Blaine noticed how she looked nervous at his arrival, not pleased, like she had been in the cemetery at their last visit.

"Neither was I," Blaine said, sounding somewhat blank. He stood quietly for a moment, adjusting to the reality that he had once again just traveled through time by no will of his own. Her seeming reluctance to see him was not the only difference on this visit. Penelope was not alone. Sitting quietly near the window was a young woman, a servant by her dress. Blaine, still standing near the closed library door, stood speechless as their eyes met. Penelope quickly took control of the situation.

"Chloe, may I present Mr. Duncan. Mr. Duncan, this is my personal servant, Chloe."

Both Blaine and Chloe nodded to one another but remained silent.

Penelope spoke quickly. "You see, Mr. Duncan, Chloe saw you at our last visit. It was necessary to take her into my confidence and explain everything that has thus far occurred. Chloe has sworn her discretion to me. However, your timing couldn't be worse for this visit. My husband shall be arriving very shortly. He must not see you." She turned to Chloe and said, "Busy yourself outside this room and ensure the other staff or the children do not enter here. Mr. Duncan's visits are quite brief. Perhaps we will not be discovered."

"Yes, Ma'am," Chloe replied, casting a look of suspicion Blaine's way before exiting the library.

"I'm sorry," Blaine said, after Chloe left the room. "I don't seem to have any control over when this happens."

"I understand, Mr. Duncan. Perhaps we should keep our voices low. The music will cover our conversation."

Penelope began playing again. Blaine moved to a chair near the piano.

"I'm afraid I have no way of explaining your presence if we were to be discovered," Penelope was saying. "We are quite isolated here in the manor. It is several miles to the trading post, and there is no horse or carriage to explain your arrival."

"I'm sorry," Blaine said again. "I have no desire to make trouble for you. Is there a way out of here without being seen?"

"I'm afraid not; only the way you came."

The piano suddenly fell silent as they both heard the sound of the carriage approaching. Blaine could hear a man's voice call out to unseen others to collect Mr. Burke's baggage and see to the horses and carriage. Only an instant later, the sound of children beyond the library door were calling "Father is home," as they ran to the carriage entry behind the library. At that same instant Chloe poked her head in the barely open library door with a panicked whisper. "The Master is home, Ma'am. What shall I do?"

"I shall be there momentarily. Do not let anyone enter here," she said, quickly rising from her place at the piano.

Blaine's eyes quickly scanned the room looking for a place to hide. Aside from slipping behind one of the thick drapes that hung at the windows, there was none.

"Keep still," Penelope cautioned as she slipped into the great room, and then he was alone.

Blaine stood still a moment considering all the ways this could play out. The best case scenario would be for him to simply vanish back to his own time. Sadly, he could not make that happen on his own. He moved to one of the windows to see if he might make an exit there. They would not open. Even if he could get outside the house, the number of men outside greatly reduced his chances of getting away unseen. Like an amateur thief in a B-rated movie, he opted for the flimsy cover of the drapes and slipped in behind one, hoping he would vanish soon. He did not. He stood there listening to the sounds of Penelope, her children and staff as they welcomed Levi Burke home. Blaine felt like a secret lover who had been hidden away from a dangerously jealous husband. Yet, he and Penelope had done no wrong. They weren't even on a first name basis. Still, this was the 1600's. Adultery was a considerably more serious offense in this time than in his. Penelope could be in serious danger if he were discovered. He suddenly froze as he heard the library door open quietly.

"Mr. Duncan?" he heard his name whispered, "Are you still here?"

It was Chloe. Blaine peeked out from behind the drape. "I'm here," he said, feeling a bit like a guilty child.

Chloe wrinkled her nose at the sight of him cowering behind the drapes. "Everyone has gathered in the parlor. I am instructed to let you out the side entrance where you can conceal yourself in the trees beyond. We must go quietly."

Blaine fell in behind Chloe as they stepped into the great room. He was momentarily distracted by the elegance of it all: the flawless marble floors and matching marble pillars; the rich rugs, tapestries and grand furnishings far exceeding their counterpart in his time. As they were about to turn into the carriageway entry, the parlor doors opened and Levi Burke stepped into the great room in time to see Blaine and Chloe. Everyone stopped.

Levi Burke eyed Blaine's clothing, clearly inadequate to the time. Blaine knew he must look like a pauper.

Levi scowled. "Chloe! Who is this vagabond in my home?"

At the sound of his stern question, Penelope rushed to the great room to stand beside her husband. Chloe's eyes widened in fear. She looked at Levi, then Penelope and back again. Blaine stood motionless.

"Answer me, Chloe," Levi roared.

Penelope didn't know what to do. She stood there in silence, hoping this would not be the moment Mr. Duncan disappeared. Chloe lifted a hand to gesture toward Blaine as though she was going to introduce him. As she did so, and before she could speak, Blaine vanished. Chloe, Penelope and Levi each gasped, but each for a different reason.

Penelope had no idea how she would explain this or what Levi would do when she did. Chloe was not shocked by his disappearance, but feared she may be asked to betray Penelope with an explanation. But Levi's gasp was one of pure astonishment; an astonishment that would soon be followed by a most terrifying conclusion. One that neither Penelope nor Chloe had ever considered and one that would have ramifications across time.

CHAPTER 11

Blaine suddenly found himself back home, away from Chloe, Penelope and Levi Burke. He leaned against the wall in the great room running his fingers through his hair in panic. He had left Penelope and Chloe in a bad situation and he was helpless to do anything about it. He had no idea how Levi would respond to his disappearance, but he felt certain it would not be good.

"Dammit!" He yelled to the ceiling. "Whoever you are that's doing this, you just made a mess of things!"

To his astonishment, there came a reply to his angry words.

"You are quite correct, Blaine. I'm afraid I have."

The voice was as clear as if its owner was standing next to him, but he saw no one. The voice continued. "Meet me upstairs and I shall attempt to explain."

Blaine rubbed his head as though he were trying to clear

it. Was he losing his mind now and hearing voices that weren't there?

"Upstairs!" the voice said again with a new firmness.

Blaine took the stairs obediently and when he reached the top, the voice called out again. "In here," it said, coming from the master suite.

As he entered the room, he saw a very old man in long robes of deep blue. His hair was long and white, as was his beard. Pale blue eyes looked out from beneath heavy white brows. Blaine stood frozen near the entry.

"Who are you?" he asked.

"I think you know the answer to that," the old man said softly.

"Are you the one who's been doing this?" Blaine asked angrily.

"I am."

"Do you know what you've done?" he said, his anger growing by the moment.

The old man lowered his eyes and sighed. "It wasn't supposed to happen this way. I failed to take Mr. Burke's part into account. A great error, I admit, but we can correct this if we work together."

"We! What do you mean 'we'? I've had no say in this since the beginning. Just who and what are you?"

"I am a timekeeper."

"A timekeeper! What the hell is that?"

"Just what it sounds like. We keepers are not supposed to

show ourselves to mortals under normal circumstances, however, I believe this calls for an exception."

"You mean, you screwed up and now you need my help to fix it."

"You are an insightful man, Mr. Duncan."

"Who gave you the right to mess with people's lives and hurl them back and forth through time?"

"I can't say exactly who gave me the right; only that I have it. It's what timekeepers do. We keep time within designated boundaries. Burkeshire Manor is within my boundaries. As for "hurling people back and forth through time" as you so vulgarly put it, it was for both yours and Penelope's good. You needed each other. I simply accommodated that. But now, well, there's a bit of a fly in the ointment, as you mortals put it. Look around, Mr. Duncan," he said, waving his arms toward the walls of the room.

Blaine had been so angry and focused on the timekeeper that he failed to notice the paintings were gone. Not one remained to mark his past and future visits.

"The paintings! Where did they go?"

"Well, there's the fly, as it were. They no longer exist. Neither does the journal found by your friend Jack and his friend Gabe. It's all gone. Because of today's journey into the past, the future has been changed, and we—you and I—need to set things right."

"Wait a minute. You're the timekeeper. Can't you just change things yourself?"

"I cannot. You see, I gave you and Penelope Burke time. But you and all mortals are beings of free will. Naturally, when I do this for two people such as you and Penelope, I assess your personalities and tendencies well before hand. Having done that, I concluded that you would make the most of this opportunity. Sadly, I did not assess Mr. Burke well enough and his response to today was, well, let's just say, the fly in the ointment."

Blaine forgot his anger for a moment and became very concerned about Penelope and Chloe. "What's he going to do to them," he asked.

"Nothing, if we can fix this," the timekeeper said, "but if not, well, Mr. Burke will decide that Cloe and his wife have been dabbling in witchcraft and he will have them both burned to death and their ashes flung into the sea. You will never travel back through time and meet her. Jack will never be your best friend, and let's just say, your future will not look very bright."

"But I have traveled back in time to meet her. How can you say that won't happen?"

"It's complicated, Mr. Duncan. You and I both know you have travel through time because I have let you retain your memories of the correct timeline so that you may assist me. But truthfully, in this timeline, you have not traveled at all. Consequently, you cannot discuss any of this with Jack or anyone else. You and I are the only ones who know how things are supposed to be."

Blaine was too overwhelmed to be angry anymore. All he could say was, "How do we fix this now?"

"For the time being I have some planning to do. You must continue on here until I return, as though nothing has happened. Here and now, in this timeline, you are Blaine Michael Duncan, widower, trying to fulfill your wife's dream here at the manor. You have hired some help as before, but your relationship with Jack is limited to his taking you to the hospital and that first night here after her death. He did not pursue a friendship with you beyond that night. Can you manage that for now?"

"I suppose I have no choice," he said, and only thought the word "*again*".

"I dare not give you your memories specific to this timeline. The need to set things right is too important. Having both sets of memories may inadvertently create another paradox. You'll just have to "wing it" as your people say. Now, I must leave you to begin planning this endeavor. I will return shortly."

With that, the timekeeper simply drifted from view, like a puff of vapor, into nothingness. Blaine imagined it was similar to what Penelope had seen each time he had returned from her time to his.

Blaine sank down on the bed, staring at the blank walls where the paintings had been. He tried to gather his thoughts. A timekeeper! He had never considered such a possibility. But then again, he never thought he would experience time travel either. In an odd sort of way, it made sense there would be someone in charge of such things.

He considered what the timekeeper had said about Levi

Burke believing his wife and Chloe to be witches. Yes. The years 1692 and 1693 were the years of the Salem witch trials. Women and some men were considered to be witches when circumstances were unable to be explained in any other way. Some were hanged, others burned at the stake. But that was in Salem, nowhere near the manor in Maine. He thought a moment. Levi Burke had returned this day, but from where? Blaine concluded that he must travel for business and his business must have been in Massachusetts. There, he would have been aware of the witch trials and maybe even seen one. He realized that when he vanished today from the Burke home, Levi would have almost no explanation other than witchcraft.

He groaned under the realization of the two women's impending fate. The timekeeper had said Levi Burke would have them burned and their ashes flung into the sea.

"Oh, my God," he moaned as this realization hit him. "What have we done? What have we done?"

It was nearing 9 p.m., too late to see the cemetery without a flashlight, but he grabbed a flashlight and went anyway. He had to see what had changed. The first, most obvious difference was Penelope Burke's grave. It was not there. Upon further investigation he found that Chloe's grave was missing as well, as where the four children. Mr. Burke's and the remaining house staff's graves were still there, as were the three small graves of the infants who had died shortly after their birth.

He decided the next day he would drive into town to check the house's history at the library. Maybe that would tell him more about what happened. He also thought he would go to the antique stores and hardware stores to feel out the relationships that currently existed between him and the owners. This could get tricky. It occurred to him that getting a few back issues of the local paper might clue him into what's been going on in Machias Bay recently.

Sleep was a near impossibility that night. All he could do was lie awake and think of the horrible fate that awaited Penelope Burke and her dear friend Chloe. Even though he couldn't have changed a thing, he still felt as though he was somehow to blame. He simply couldn't get his head around all that had happened. It was nearly 3 a.m. before he finally drifted off for only a few hours of sleep.

CHAPTER 12

Levi Burke's mind tried to absorb what he had just witnessed. The shoddy-looking stranger had just vanished before his eyes. From where he stood, it appeared that Chloe had simply waved her hand and it had been so. It didn't take more than that for Levi's mind to return to the pub in Salem and recall the charges of witchcraft from the men in the pub. He recalled in seconds how that woman had been accused of conjuring an illness to rid herself of her family. One could conceivably question charges such as those, but making a man disappear, there could be no question. In spite of his efforts to protect his family by secreting them away in this wilderness territory, he had failed.

Faster than seemed humanly possible, Levi Burke crossed the great room and roughly seized Chloe by the arm. At the same time, he called out to Mrs. Wilmington who was still in the parlor. Mrs. Wilmington appeared in the great room beside Penelope, who was still frozen in place.

"Yes, Mr. Burke?"

"Take this woman to the cellar and lock her in," Levi commanded.

"I beg your pardon, Sir?"

"You heard me. And tie her hands."

Chloe burst into tears of fright. Penelope found her voice and rushed to intervene. "No, Levi. What are you thinking?" she cried.

Chloe look at Penelope with fear and pleading in her eyes as Levi dragged her across the room and shoved her toward Mrs. Wilmington.

"Levi, please," Penelope begged, "You must stop. Chloe has done nothing."

"Nothing!" he growled. "Nothing! Did you not see with your own eyes how she vanished a man with a wave of her hand?"

Penelope suddenly understood what Levi was thinking. Horror rose in her throat. "No! You don't understand! Chloe is innocent! Please don't do this." She was weeping nearly as hysterically as Chloe now.

Mrs. Wilmington also grasped the implication. She summoned Mr. Wilmington to assist her in confining Chloe. All the while, Chloe and Penelope were in the grip of terror and hysteria. The children stood wide-eyed at the parlor door with Millie, who was equally stunned, standing behind them. Levi ordered Millie to take the children upstairs immediately and stay there until he sent for them.

Millie quickly herded the children toward the stairs. The girls were in tears over the spectacle. 12-year-old Alex did not cry, but fear was clearly visible in his eyes. Not for himself, but for his mother. He felt he should protect his mother from whatever was frightening her. He broke from the girls and ran to his mother's side clutching her hand. His father saw this and misinterpreted his actions as personal fear. A boy, cowering to his mother's side. Levi himself would not admit to the fear within. It fueled his anger and he lashed out at Alex, saying, "Don't cower at your mother's side, boy. Join the other children. Now!"

His words cut Alex like a dagger. That was the last time Alex would ever yearn for his father's love or approval. That was also the last day he would ever consider himself a boy. He knew his father would never understand the love he felt for his mother and sisters. He would never understand the loyalty that comes with family. Why had he ever wanted to be like his father, he suddenly wondered.

He stood his ground, glaring at his father in pure defiance until Levi finally said, "Very well, as you wish."

Penelope had stopped pleading and was now weeping silently beside her son. Things had gone so wrong, so quickly. There was no going back. She already knew there was nothing she could explain to Levi that wouldn't make things worse. She dabbed at her eyes and turned to her son.

"Alex, my dear, let's join Millie and the girls together, shall we?"

As they made their way up the great sweeping staircase, Levi was left alone with his thoughts. He paced, one hand grasping his waistcoat, the other rubbing his brow as he considered what to do next. He considered his words to Buckman in Salem. "I don't believe God can do anything for me that I cannot do for myself. I would wager I am equally independent of the devil's will. However, I have no wish to test the strength of those words should the need arise."

He believed those words still, yet now he knew that need had come to put them to the test. Evil had come to his home in spite of his efforts to isolate his family. He and Penelope had trusted Chloe with their children these many years. He hoped she had not had sufficient time to compromise their souls. He also remembered the words of the men in the pub saying it was not enough to hang a witch, she must be burned. He knew that banishing this witch to the next world would be a crushing blow to Penelope. The two had developed a close bond that Penelope would not forsake unless she fully understood. He must tell her. Help her to understand the threat Chloe was to them all. And, he must do it now, before the witch could strike again.

Levi moved up the stairs toward Penelope's room. It saddened him to have to do this to someone his young wife held so dear, but in time she would understand that he was doing what he must for her and the children.

Levi had rarely entered Penelope's room. He had respected her need for privacy and he knew she was sensitive about her paintings, never believing her work was adequate for public viewing. He rapped softly on the door. There was no reply. He knocked again, calling her name as he did. Once again, there was no reply. He quietly turned the knob and pushed the door open. She was nowhere to be seen. He decided she must be in the children's room with Millie. He was about to leave and look for her with the children when a painting on the easel caught his eye. He walked to the easel for a closer look. It was the painting of the cemetery. Not just the cemetery, but Penelope was there along with a young man. Levi's breath caught in his throat. It was the same young man he'd seen today. He and Penelope appeared to be conversing. Levi turned to the multitude of paintings that stood against the wall. One by one he went through them until he found what he was looking for. Three more paintings depicting Penelope with the young man. One more from the cemetery looking up to see him in the window of the master suite, one in Penelope's room and one with the man seated at the top of the stairs. Levi needed to brace himself against the wall as the wave of dizziness nearly caused him to black out. The implications were staggering. At best, his wife had betrayed him with this man. At worst she had been complicit in witchcraft to hide her betrayal.

Levi could not distinguish between his grief and his rage. He was consumed as he made his way to the children's room. In his arms were the four paintings with their immutable testimony of betrayal. When he reached the children's room it was all he could do to remain calm as he motioned for Penelope to join him in the hallway. Penelope quickly complied as she saw he was holding four of her paintings in his arms. Her heart was pounding so fiercely she feared it would burst at any moment. She did not want another scene in front of the children. She stepped into the hallway and closed the door behind her. She could see that no amount of explanation would help her now. Levi's own interpretation was plainly visible in his eyes and in the silently fierce set of his face.

A few moments later she found herself bound and resting beside Chloe in the dark cellar. The two huddled together weeping.

"I'm so sorry, Chloe," she cried. "I never should have involved you in this. Please forgive me... Please forgive me..."

News of the man who vanished had spread through the servants, both men and women. The women sat silently weeping in the kitchen, except for Millie, who was upstairs with the children. Mr. Burke had gone outside to speak privately with Mr. Wilmington. When he returned to the kitchen his face appeared to have aged ten years since his return earlier that evening.

To Mrs. Wilmington, he said, "Take the women upstairs and prepare the children and their belongings for travel. They will be returning to Boston with me tomorrow. My man will carry you to the harbor this night where you shall be given accommodations for the night. I shall join you in the morning and take charge of the children and you shall return here. Is that perfectly clear?"

"Yes, Mr. Burke," Mrs. Wilmington said through her tears. She ushered the other women out of the kitchen to carry out her instructions.

"You shall be ready to leave in one hour," he called after her.

Though Chloe had continued quietly weeping, Penelope sat silently now in the blackness. She was resigned to her fate, just as she had always been. For whatever reason, she had been consigned to a loveless marriage with a man nearly twice her age, and locked away from everyone and everything she had known. She had tried to accept this with grace and dignity. And though she had indeed been blessed with children she loved more than life, she had learned to live without personal happiness.

Now, when she had finally begun to hope that her patience would be rewarded with a new companionship, it, instead, became her downfall. Nevertheless, she had only two regrets. Leaving her children behind, and taking Chloe down with her.

How she longed to hold her children once more and make certain they knew how deeply and eternally she loved them, but there was nothing she could do. However, she thought there might still be a chance she could save Chloe. When Levi came for them she would declare that she alone was the witch and in spite of how it may have appeared, it was Penelope herself that had vanished the man. She would proclaim Chloe's innocence in hopes of saving her. But Chloe would need to cooperate.

Though the blackness of the cellar prevented them from actually seeing one another, Penelope turned her face in Chloe's direction. "Chloe, listen to me closely. When Mr. Burke comes for us, I want you to remain silent. I will explain that I alone am guilty of conjuring and that you are innocent. You must let me do this, my dear friend. My soul shall never rest knowing I have brought such wickedness down upon your head."

Chloe was silent except for the quiet whimpering.

"Chloe. Tell me you will do this. I cannot bear the burden of your death."

Chloe leaned in closer to Penelope and whispered, "And I cannot live without you in this house and bear the burden of yours. I shall remain at your side."

When Mrs. Wilmington, the driver and children had left, Levi instructed the other men to begin preparation. He ordered a wagonload of firewood to be brought out to the cliffs beyond the cemetery as well as wagon wheel grease to propel the flames. He further ordered ropes and shovels to be loaded into the wagon. Only Mr. Wilmington had been told how and why this must be done, but with the earlier talk of witchcraft among the servants, it wasn't difficult to determine the purpose of their orders. Not one of the men was comfortable with the task at hand, but they had been serving Mr. Burke for many years. Disobeying his orders was not considered an option, and none wished to be considered conspirators by their disobedience.

The horses pulled the wagon to the chosen location while

the men walked alongside. Only Mr. Wilmington returned to the house to assist Mr. Burke in bringing Penelope and Chloe to the cliffs.

It was May 20, 1693. The hour was near midnight. The full moon obscured some of the brightness of the stars. The air was comfortable this spring night and surprisingly still. Very little breeze blew in from the ocean.

As Penelope and Chloe walked in quiet resolution toward the cliffs, Penelope thought how beautiful it was here in spite of her loneliness. Mr. Burke and Mr. Wilmington held each of them by the arm. Their wrists were still tied in front of them. Neither wept. Neither spoke. When they reached the others, the men took the women to a small tree at the edge of the cliffs. Their hands were untied so that they could be bound back to back against the tree. Bundles of firewood were loaded around their feet and swathed in oil.

Penelope worked her hand backward under the ropes that bound them until she found Chloe's hand. She wrapped her fingers around Chloe's and whispered, "I love you, my dear Chloe."

When all was ready, Levi, himself lit the torch and raised it high in the air. "It grieves me to find witchery in my own home, and to find my own wife conspiring with such evil. Nevertheless, it is my duty to cleanse my own house, for God has not seen fit to do so." He then turned to Penelope. "May God forgive you, for I cannot."

With those words, he let the torch fall. The wheel grease

spread the flames quickly. Silent tears for Chloe and for her children slid down Penelope's cheeks, but neither woman cried out. As the flames grew higher and higher, Penelope whispered, "Save us, Mr. Duncan. Save us."

A moment later both women were concealed in flames. The smell of burning flesh sickened more than one of the men and they turned away in revulsion. Levi alone stood in silence watching the horrific spectacle, and when he was certain his face could no longer be seen by the other men, he let go the tears that filled his eyes.

CHAPTER 13

It was nearly 3 a.m. when Blaine finally drifted off to sleep. Before he slept, his mind kept playing back the words of the timekeeper. Levi Burke had decided Chloe and Penelope had used witchcraft to conjure him and then to vanish him. For this crime they would be burned as witches. And all the while, Blaine would be safe in the future.

He felt helpless and dirty for his part in their fate. It was as though he was guilty of this horrific murder himself. When he finally slept out of sheer exhaustion, he was tormented by dreams of fire consuming him in a never ending blaze. He could feel the flames licking his skin and see his flesh, black and falling, but was denied the mercy of dying. The dream seemed to go on endlessly. When he finally awoke with a start before sunrise, he was soaked in sweat. The sheets were wrapped tightly around him like ropes that bound him. He struggled in a panic to free himself of the bed sheets and scrambled to sit up for fear he would fall back into the dream and be trapped once again.

The room was well lit with light from the full moon outside his window. Instinctively, he took a moment to clear his head enough to insure he was in his own time. He appeared to be, but with that realization came the recollection of Penelope's and Chloe's fate. He pulled himself up to sit on the edge of his bed, trying to drive the dream from his head. It was then that he heard her voice. It sounded soft at first, barely audible, and not right. It was filled with a kind of quiet terror, a desperate pleading and finally, hopelessness.

"Save us, Mr. Duncan. Save us."

His eyes quickly scanned the room, looking for the source of the voice, yet deep in his heart he knew who had spoken. He knew her voice well. It was Penelope Burke. A moment later he saw her standing near the door in his room, but it was different from the times he had seen her before. She was not the living woman he had traveled to see before this. There was no mistaking it. She was a spirit. A ghost, if you will. Her eyes held fear and pleading as she repeated her words. "Save us." An instant later she was being consumed in flames. He saw agony in her face as the flames took her. Blaine was sickened to discover this was more than just an encounter. The foul odor of burning flesh filled the room causing his stomach to heave involuntarily. He cried out to dispel the ungodly vision before him but to no avail. There was nothing he could do. The flames engulfed her until there was nothing but fire. An instant later the entire image was gone, but the sickening smell of burning flesh remained.

Blaine groaned in futility. "No!" He cried again and again. "No! No! No! I can't bear this. You must change this," he cried into the night. "She can't die like this! Do you hear me? I know you can hear me, you bastard! Change this, now!" His voice trailed off in agony.

Though he'd had little sleep, he could not risk another dream. He staggered to the bathroom and turned on the shower. He stepped in without removing his shorts. He let the water run over him, clearing his head and pushing away the smell of burning flesh. He wondered if this was what the timekeeper had meant when he said his future would not be bright? Was he to be haunted by Penelope Burke for the rest of his life and suffer as she did in his dreams each night? Then he thought, "I guess that would be some degree of justice. It's because of me that she had to die such a horrible death."

He kept hearing her words, "*Save us, Mr. Duncan,*" over and over again. But he hadn't been able to save her. He had been 300 years away, unable to do anything. He remembered how she had told him that day they walked the cliffs how she was hoping he could help her. But all he had done was insure a most horrific death for her and Chloe. How would he live with that for the rest of his life? He couldn't. It would drive him insane. Where was the timekeeper? There had to be a way to fix this.

Though it was only 5 a.m., he dragged himself downstairs

after his shower and started some coffee. A couple of strong cups should get him going. It certainly seemed like a better option than sleep. As he went through the motions of morning, in the back of his mind, the words kept repeating, *"We've got to change this,"* over and over again.

No matter how hard he tried, he couldn't shake the image of Penelope's face as she pleaded with him to save her. He decided he couldn't stay in this house today. He had to do something to figure this out. The timekeeper had not returned since yesterday and there was no way of knowing when he would be back.

Blaine decided he would start at the library in town and see what he could dig up on the events that happened at Burkeshire Manor. He wasn't sure how it would help, but he had to do something or he would go crazy. Unfortunately, the library wouldn't be open for a few hours yet. There was an all-night diner at the truck stop just outside of town. At least there was in the other timeline. He decided he would go there to wait.

By 5:30 he was in his truck and on the road. It was about a fifteen minute drive and the traffic was near non-existent at this hour. As he came up on the interstate, he was relieved to see the truck stop was still where it ought to be.

He took a seat at the counter and ordered his third cup of coffee for the morning and a light breakfast of French toast to help absorb some of the acid. His mind turned to possible solutions to the nightmare of events that had taken place. He considered the evidence at hand. Had he never traveled back in time, this would never have happened. While that course of non-action may have saved Penelope's and Chloe's lives, she would still have gone on in loneliness for the rest of her life. The timekeeper had made it clear that the purpose of his sending Blaine back in time was to bring some happiness to both him and Penelope. In spite of his grumbling about not having control over his life, he had to admit he had enjoyed his brief visits with Penelope and it was clear she enjoyed his company, too. So he concluded that while never going back in the first place would save her life, it may not be the best answer. Next he began to consider that if he hadn't traveled back yesterday, Levi Burke would not have seen him and this nightmare of consequences would never have happened.

But then again, would the timekeeper be able to undo only yesterday's visit? For that matter, this could still happen again on some future visit. In that case Penelope could still be in danger at some future time. That brought his thinking back around to plan A. Just don't go back at all. Why did that idea trouble him so? He realized that if he never went back, he would miss her. Maybe the timekeeper was right. Maybe they did need each other. He went over it again and again as he sat in the diner, but couldn't figure out how to solve this.

To take his mind off it for a while, he picked up the local paper that was sitting near him on the counter. He skimmed through the local news, trying to determine if there were any significant changes in this timeline that he should be aware of, but nothing jumped out at him.

"Have trouble sleeping last night?" a man's voice asked.

Blaine looked up, a little startled by the unexpected question. At first glance he didn't recognize the man who asked the question, but he quickly determined why. It was the timekeeper, but he had changed. His long white hair and beard were now neatly trimmed to an appropriate length and his long blue robes had been replaced by a blue sports jacket and tan trousers.

He smiled as he saw recognition in Blaine's eyes. "When in Rome," he said with a wink.

Blaine was not amused. "Do you have any idea what kind of night I had?" he growled. He tried to keep his voice low as he added, "I had a visit from Penelope Burke's ghost this morning. Why haven't you fix this yet? I don't want to go through this and I don't want Penelope to die like that. What are you going to do about this?"

"Patience, Mr. Duncan. Perhaps we should take a booth. This conversation needs a little privacy."

Blaine left his plate on the counter but grabbed his coffee cup and followed the timekeeper to a booth in the rear of the diner. As they seated themselves, Blaine asked, "What do I call you anyway. Timekeeper seems a bit awkward for public situations."

"How about Timothy? Yes. Tim Keeper. I rather like that."

Blaine rolled his eyes at the obvious play on words, but he agreed it was less conspicuous than timekeeper. "Fine, Mr. Keeper."

"Oh, please, Tim."

"Okay, Tim, what are you going to do about this?"

"Well, there are many points to take into account in our plan. You can't just go changing time willy-nilly or you'll make a bigger mess than when you started. Every individual in every moment of time has his or her own impact on events. These impacts must be weighed and measured to determine what may be changed and what may not."

"You skirt around a straight question like a politician. Tell me what you decided to do and let's get on with it."

"Mr. Duncan, don't try my patience. It is critical that we act carefully. I will lay this out for you and I suggest you listen and learn. You will need to understand all that I am telling you before we begin. Is that clear?"

Blaine nodded. "You're right. I'm sorry. I'm just having a little trouble dealing with the idea that I'm talking to someone who isn't even supposed to be here about changing a timeline that isn't supposed to be happening. It's not exactly how I expected to be spending my time two days ago."

"Yes, my dear boy. I understand. Just bear with me. I have been looking at Levi Burke's life. I needed to determine when he would die in both this timeline and the original timeline."

"I don't understand," Blaine said questioningly.

"Mr. Burke was not an obscure individual. He was a man of great wealth and influence. Nearly everything he did impacted many other lives."

"In what way?"

"He was a lumber man. His mills had many employees. His company harvested many acres of timber, which, in turn, provided many landowners with means to provide for their families. And it goes on and on. If I were to remove him from his life prematurely it would create a negative impact that I may never be able to repair."

"I don't understand. What do you mean when you say 're-move him from his life'? Do you mean kill him?"

"I deal in time and time only. I am not able to terminate a mortal life."

Blaine let out a moan of understanding. "You're saying you want me to take him out. Are you crazy? I'm not a killer. You made this mistake and now you want me to do your dirty work?"

"Take it easy, Blaine. I said no such thing. I just want you to know I'm researching all possible avenues. Please try to be patient. Timekeeping is a very delicate matter. We will fix this, I promise you that. I must go now. There is much to do."

Timothy Keeper left the table and walked into the men's room. Blaine waited, until he realized he was not coming out but had only disguised his exit. Blaine paid his tab and took his time driving back to town. He parked his truck in front of the library, then settled back for a bit of much-needed sleep while he waited for it to open.

CHAPTER 14

Thankfully, he slept for the next hour and a half without dreams. When he awoke, the library was open. He made his way to the main desk and asked for Lucy, the name Jack had given him in the previous timeline.

"I'm Lucy," the woman at the desk replied, "how can I help you?"

"I'm looking for anything you have on the history of Burkeshire Manor."

"Oh, yes. You must be Mr. Duncan, the man who bought the place last year."

"Yes," Blaine said. "Do you have anything?"

"I'm sure I do. Rumor has it that place had quite a tragic history. Some folks say it's haunted," she continued, as he followed her back to the local history section. "Of course, I don't know if you believe in such things, but it adds a little color to the town's history, don't you think?"

"Yes, color," Blaine mumbled.

She fished through several titles, drawing out three books as she went. "These should give you a good start," she said, handing the books to Blaine. "Let me know if you need more."

Blaine took the books to a table in the reference section and opened the first book, <u>A History of Machias Bay</u>. He skimmed the Table of Contents for something about the manor. The only subject that looked promising was Historical Landmarks. He flipped to that section, which held many old photos with varying length descriptions. There was a photo of the manor some hundred years ago. It was in poor condition and appeared vacant. This must have been before the last renovation. He began reading historical information next to the picture.

"Burkeshire Manor was the first structure to be built in Machias Bay. Levi Burke, a wealthy businessman from Boston, began construction on this home for his wife Penelope Whittier Burke in 1678. It was completed 14 years later in 1692. The Burke family resided in the home throughout its construction. The Burke family consisted of Levi and Penelope Burke and four children, Alex, Miriam, Darcy and Ingrid. Three other children died in infancy and their graves can be found in the estate's cemetery. Little is known of the death of Penelope Burke in 1693. It was suspected she was the victim of foul play. It is a mystery why her grave does not appear in the estate's cemetery. Mr. Burke moved his children to Boston but the home

remained in the family after his death later that same year. He was
66 years old at the time of his death.

The home changed hands several times over the next 175 years.
It is said the frequently changing ownership was due in part to the
mysterious sightings of the ghosts of two women. One was believed
to be Penelope Burke and the other is unknown."

Blaine left the page open and turned to the next book.
This had a more promising title, Legends of Machias Bay. In
this book, Burkeshire Manor was the first legend recorded.
He skimmed through the story which began with much of the
same information he'd just read. At the bottom of the second
page the story caught his attention. It claimed that a man by the
name of Wilmington made a deathbed confession to his grandchildren that he had participated in the burning death of Mrs.
Penelope Burke at the behest of her husband, who believed her
and her personal maid, Chloe, to be practicing witches. His
sentence of death by fire was carried out once the children had
been removed from the home and under the cover of darkness.
Their ashes had been cast into the sea.

Blaine stifled a sob as he read these words. Suddenly the
timekeeper's words of *"removing Levi Burke from life prema-*
turely" didn't sound so crazy. How could Levi Burke murder his
wife, the mother of his children, a woman of obvious gentleness
and goodness, in this most horrifying and merciless manner?
Blaine was fuming with rage. It was all he could do to contain
his emotions in this very public place.

The third book offered little beyond what he had already

found. He asked Lucy to make copies from the two books so that he could take this information home with him.

With copies in hand, he returned home in hopes that the timekeeper might join him there. A part of him wished that the timekeeper had already made the necessary changes and he would go home to find Jack waiting for his return and thirty-three paintings hanging in the master suite. However, he was not surprised to find that that wasn't the case when he arrived.

Though it was only late morning, he pulled a beer from the fridge and walked out to the cemetery. He stood at Christina's grave in silence. Here, in this timeline as well, he had not yet completed the final task of ordering a headstone. He knew at least a part of his reluctance to do so was in knowing exactly what he wanted the epitaph to read. It had to be something special, something that would cause those who read it to ponder. Something that said how special Christina was and always would be to those who loved her.

He walked to the graves of Penelope's children, wishing she would suddenly be there to offer words of comfort, but he was alone. He raised his eyes to the ocean beyond the cliffs. After a moment he decided to walk where he and Penelope had walked on the cliffs beyond the cemetery. As he made his way farther and farther, he saw the silhouette of a person some fifty yards off, standing at the edge of the cliffs. He quickened his pace to draw closer. As he bridged the gap between them, he saw that it was a young woman. She turned to look at him when she heard his approach.

"I'm sorry. I hope I'm not trespassing," she said.

Blaine stood momentarily stunned. She was the image of Penelope. He was speechless.

"Sir? Are you all right?"

"Yes, yes. It's just that I thought you were… someone else."

"My name is Melissa Sturgis. I wasn't sure where the property boundaries were and I wanted to see the place. I hope I didn't trespass."

Blaine gathered himself enough to say, "No, you're fine."

"Good. You see, I've been making a record of my family history, and several generations back my great, great grandmother, Penelope Burke first lived in that house." She pointed in the direction of the manor. "I'm a direct descendent of her son, Alex. I've been told I look like her from old paintings."

"Indeed you do," he said, without thinking.

"Oh, have you seen old paintings of her?" she asked.

"Only in the town library," he said, covering his tracks. "I'm Blaine Duncan. Would you like to see the inside?"

"That would be wonderful, if it wouldn't be an inconvenience."

"No inconvenience," Blaine said as they fell into step together. As foolish as he knew it was, having Penelope's granddaughter beside him brought a small bit of comfort. Her likeness to Penelope was much greater than he thought she realized.

"How long have you owned the place?" she was asking.

"My wife and I bought it last year. Our plan was to turn it into a bed and breakfast within the year, but she died about six months ago in an auto accident."

"I'm so sorry to hear that."

"Thank you. I've been plugging along with our plan, but I'm afraid there's a lot left to do. Don't expect too much."

"I'm just grateful for the opportunity to go inside. This is very kind of you."

When they reached the house, Blaine took her in the front door rather than the kitchen. As they entered, she stopped to take in the huge entry.

"This is amazing. I've only seen photographs of the outside of the manor until today."

"Well, it's not as lavish on the inside as it was in its early days," Blaine said. "I understand this floor and the pillars were polished marble back then. The floor plan has remained about the same though, except for adding plumbing and electric and bathrooms." He seemed to have caught a spark of her enthusiasm. "C'mon, I'll show you the rest of the place."

He showed her through the rooms of the main floor, then led her upstairs. He stayed in the hall as he opened each door to let her look inside.

"My wife and I took the master suite for now until the work is done. Once we opened for business, we planned to turn the guest house into our place. Sorry about the mess in there. I wasn't expecting company."

"So this is where my grandmother slept."

Once again Blaine didn't stop to think when he said, "Actually, she only slept here when her husband was home. Her room is just down the hall."

Melissa looked at Blaine quizzically. "How would you know that?" she asked.

Blaine tried to sound nonchalant as he explained, "Well, that was customary in the 1600s for those of wealth. The master and mistress often had separate rooms. That's what I've read anyway."

He could tell his explanation was met with some reservation, but Melissa didn't pursue it further.

"There are more bedrooms on the third floor, but they haven't been done yet." He showed her the room he had declared to be Penelope's room and the remaining bedroom and bath on the second level. As they came down the stairs, he asked if she would like a cup of coffee. He sensed that his comment about Penelope's room had made her ill at ease.

"Thank you, no. I think I should head back to my car. It's back where we met. I would like to come back tomorrow, if it's all right with you, to get some outside shots of the house."

"I don't see why not. I'll be here all day."

"Thank you again. I'll just let myself out."

Blaine stopped to consider what had just happened. Melissa was Penelope's great, great granddaughter. That meant that even with Penelope's death, her son Alex grew up, married and had at least one child. He pulled another beer out and sat down at the kitchen table with his copies from the library.

"What are the odds that I would run into Penelope's great, great, etc., granddaughter? I wonder if the same thing was going to happen in the other timeline. She probably thinks I'm some kind of a nut job the way I was talking today. I'm surprised she wants to come back at all. Hell, with any luck this day won't even happen, or, we can do it all again only better the next time."

Blaine took a long swig of beer. "This must be what it feels like when someone starts to go crazy. Talking to myself. Considering possibilities I would never have imagined a week ago. Yeah, we've got to fix this—and soon."

There was one potentially positive find at the library today. According to the information he had gathered, Levi Burke died later the same year he murdered his wife. That meant it was unlikely he had much time to make any significant impact after Penelope's death. He hated his next thought, but it had to be considered. Maybe he *should* be removed from his life sooner rather than later. He certainly deserved it for what he was going to do. I don't care what century you live in. You don't get to make yourself judge, jury and executioner simply because you don't understand what's happening. Where the hell was that timekeeper?

CHAPTER 15

A moment later, Blaine found himself looking at the time-keeper who had suddenly appeared in his kitchen. There was a look of annoyance on his face.

"I thought we agreed you would call me Tim. And I think it's time to drop the hostility you've been sending my way and realize that we're aiming for the same goal. I've been a time-keeper for more centuries than I care to admit. This is the first complication I've faced. Can you say that about your life?"

Blaine was still adjusting to the fact that Timothy had just materialized in the kitchen. Responding to everything he just said took a moment. Finally he spoke. "Fair enough." He raised his bottle in a gesture of conciliation. "So, how's the research going?"

"As you already know, Levi Burke died a short time after his wife. He had a heart attack. To be precise, and I must be, his death occurred 67 days later. The children were raised by one Esther Reese who ran a boarding house in Boston. This is where Levi brought them until he could make more permanent arrangements. Esther was a kindhearted woman. She raised them with love as best she could.

More importantly, after considerable research, I have found that Levi Burke must live those 67 days. There are two events that must take place or the future for many others will be altered severely, including Penelope's children. The first event is that he must bring the children to Boston. It's the only way to conceal the temporary disappearance of their mother. The second event is business related. The details of that are of no interest to you."

"Wait! You said the temporary disappearance of their mother. Not the death of their mother? Does that mean you have a plan?"

"I believe I do, but we must orchestrate this with meticulous precision. And I do mean 'we'. I'm going to need your help with this. Are you willing to do that?"

"If it will keep that monster husband of hers from murdering her; yes. What do I need to do?"

"First I must show you exactly what happened that night. It will be painful for you, but you must know what will happen ahead of time. We can't do this if you don't have your emotions under control, and you won't when you see it for the first time. Consider it a rehearsal."

Blaine considered what the timekeeper was telling him. He

would have to watch the horror of Penelope's and Chloe's death without the ability to step in and help them. Could he handle that? He would have to.

"Will they know we're there?" Blaine asked.

"No. You will be in my realm, out of time, as it were. We will witness everything, but no one will see or hear us."

"So when we do this for real, what will happen?"

"We must allow Levi to think he killed his wife and her maid. This is where precision timing comes in. After he has set the flames, I shall take Penelope and Chloe out of time momentarily and replace them with two women who were previously burned as witches in Salem earlier that year. Those women were already meant to die. The switch will not interfere with the timeline."

"Then, where will I be?"

"You will be waiting in the trees near the cliffs. I will deliver Penelope and Chloe to you there. You must keep them quiet and safe until the men have finished with the aftermath."

"Then, what?"

"Then you must explain to them why they must return here to your time. They must remain here for 67 days, until Levi Burke has died. Only then can they return. Penelope may then rejoin her children and live out her life at Burkeshire Manor as she was meant to."

Blaine was impressed. "That just may work."

"It will work if we both do our part. There will be some minor changes from the original timeline. Penelope and Chloe will remember these events. That means her journal entries will be somewhat different as well some of the paintings you find, but nothing significant enough to alter the timeline. Everything will be as it was meant to be."

Blaine leaned back in his chair. "I met her granddaughter today, several generations removed."

The timekeeper smiled. "And you will again. If everything goes well, Penelope will meet her as well."

That brought a smile to Blaine's lips, but it vanished quickly when the timekeeper said, "Prepare yourself, Blaine. It's time to go."

A moment later, Blaine found himself standing beside the timekeeper on the cliffs beyond the cemetery. It was night, but he could see everything as clearly as if it were day. He saw the wagon loaded with firewood, shovels and rope. He saw Burke's men standing by, waiting for instructions. Then he saw Levi Burke and Mr. Wilmington leading Penelope and Chloe towards them. The women's hands were bound. For a moment he wanted to tell the timekeeper he couldn't do this, but he knew he had to. He watched as the women's bonds were removed only to be replaced with ropes used to tie them to the tree at the edge of the cliffs. Though they stood some distance away, Blaine could hear every utterance of the men, every breath that was taken, with crystal clarity. It was as though every one of his senses were magnified. He saw Penelope's hand struggle under the ropes to reach Chloe's hand. Then he heard her whisper "I love you, my dear Chloe." Finally, he heard the words of condemnation from Levi Burke as he held the torch high. For a while, there were no more words from Levi or any of the men. Levi dropped the torch and Blaine watched as the flames took hold. But when Penelope whispered too quietly for anyone else to hear her, "Save us, Mr. Duncan. Save us," Blaine heard her clearly. He couldn't contain himself anymore. Those were the same words she had said in his room early this morning when she appeared as a ghost. The same words she had likely been saying for the 300 years she had haunted the manor since this night. The flames had reached them and quickly devoured them. Blaine fell to his knees, weeping helplessly. He never thought he was capable of hating anyone as much as he hated Levi Burke at that moment. No one should die in this manner, except, maybe those who would do this to another person.

"Take me back! Take me back! I can't watch anymore!"

The timekeeper knew he had seen enough. It was time to go home.

Blaine was still on his knees when they both suddenly appeared back in the kitchen. He couldn't control the sobs of anguish he felt at what he had just witnessed.

"Kill him, Timothy," he cried. "That bastard has no right to live after what he just did."

"I'm sorry I had to put you through that. It was necessary. Just remember that she will never have to endure that again."

"She should never have had to go through it at all," he said, still trying to calm himself. Finally, as he began to calm down, he asked, "Will she remember the pain?"

"No. There will be no pain. I will take them out of time before the flames reach them and exchange them with those who were meant to die. In the darkness, no one will be the wiser."

"But those other women, they will be burned again."

"Their bodies will burn again. Their souls will already be long gone. Now, I want you to rest. You barely slept last night and you've just experienced an emotional trauma. I need you awake and alert when we return."

"How can I sleep after what I've just seen?"

"I will help you. I will keep time from you for several hours. That means no dreams, no interruption."

Blaine suddenly found himself lying in his bed, with the timekeeper standing beside him.

"Now, close your eyes. I will come for you when you are sufficiently rested."

CHAPTER 16

That was the last thing he remembered. The next thing he knew he was waking up at the same moment he had gone to sleep, but he felt more rested than he had in weeks. The timekeeper stood waiting where he had been before.

"I feel great," Blaine said. "You should bottle that. You could make a fortune."

"What would I do with a fortune? Are you ready to do this?"

"I guess so."

"Remember, you won't be out of time this trip. You can be seen and heard, so stay hidden in the trees until I deliver them to you."

"Understood. Let's go. No. Wait. Will I see you again after this?"

Timothy smiled. "If all goes well, no, you won't. But I will be watching."

"One more thing. If I am to continue traveling back through time, can I at least choose when?"

"I will consider it. Just remember, I can see the whole picture while you cannot. I must protect you and the timeline. Now, we must go."

An instant later, Blaine had returned to the fateful scene of Penelope's death; however, he was now concealed in the trees a short distance away. Unlike the last visit, he was able to see, but not hear the voices of the men or Levi Burke clearly. Further, the darkness hampered his view to a degree. Nevertheless, he knew what was happening. He had witnessed it with clarity only a short time ago. When Levi dropped the torch, Blaine readied himself. He watched as the wheel grease quickly spread the flames.

"Now, Timothy," he said, anxiously. "It has to be now."

Suddenly he found Penelope and Chloe standing back to back within inches of him. He flung his arms around both of them and quickly said, "Shhhh… you must stay quiet. It's me, Blaine Duncan."

He pulled back so they could see his face in the darkness of the trees. Recognition sparked in their eyes.

"I knew you would help us," Penelope whispered, at the same time drawing Chloe close to her. "It's all right Chloe. We'll be safe now."

"We must wait here until the men leave. Then I will explain everything. For now, just stay still and quiet."

The three of them huddled together, Chloe still trembling in fear, and watching the unholy scene before them.

"I don't understand, Sir," Chloe whispered. "Are those our bodies in the fire?"

"They are not your bodies. No one will die here tonight. Now, please keep quiet. I will explain later."

Penelope watched her husband standing firmly, facing the blaze, while the other men turned away. She had always known their marriage was not founded on love, but Levi had always treated her with kindness and gentleness. She would not have believed he would ever do her harm. "He's so afraid," she whispered under her breath. "Afraid of what he does not understand." Fear can be the root of such evil works. She almost felt a level of compassion for him. How tragic it was to see an otherwise kind man becomes someone she didn't know, because of fear.

After a long while, the flames died. They watched as Levi's men used shovels to toss every last bit of ash over the cliff and into the sea. Finally, when it was done, all returned to the manor. Blaine, Chloe and Penelope let out a collective sigh of relief. Blaine was now ready to explain as both women waited eagerly to know what was happening and what was next.

"Mr. Duncan," Penelope said humbly, "we owe you our lives. How will we ever repay you?"

Blaine shrank from her gratitude. He felt completely

undeserving of it. If it hadn't been for his untimely visit, they would not have needed saving in the first place.

"It wasn't me," he said. "I'll try to explain this, but we must hurry. You see, when I got back to my time today, I knew I had left you in a bad situation. I was angry at whomever or whatever was making this happen. I began yelling at that unknown someone, hoping he was really controlling this and listening. I screamed at him, saying that he had left you in a terrible situation and did he know what he had done. It was just irrational, angry ranting. Then it happened. I heard someone talking to me, answering me. At first I just thought I was losing my mind and hearing things that weren't there, but the voice told me to go upstairs to the master suite so that we could talk, so I did. That's when I finally saw who was speaking to me. He called himself a timekeeper. He said it was his job to keep time within his assigned boundaries. He also told me that he and other timekeepers didn't normally show themselves to us mortals, but that something had gone wrong. He told me what Levi planned to do to the two of you and how we had to stop it. You were not meant to die like this, neither of you. He said he needed my help to change this timeline and return it to the way things were meant to be. He's the one who took you from the fire and brought you here to me."

Blaine was not surprised to find Penelope accepted this explanation without hesitation, but she did have questions. He supposed that anyone who had already accepted and been comfortable with time travel would find the idea of a time-keeper not that much of a stretch.

Penelope was concerned, however. "Did saving us come at the cost of other lives? I clearly saw two women in the fire."

"The bodies you saw burning were not living. Timothy, that's the timekeeper, took the two of you out of time briefly to deliver you to me. He replaced you with the bodies of two women who had already died as they were meant to. Their souls were already passed and gone. No one died here tonight. Still, Mr. Burke must be allowed to believe that you died. By morning, he will take the children back to Boston with him. There he will place them with a kind woman who runs a boarding house until he's able to make more permanent arrangements."

Penelope felt a sob rise in her throat at the thought of her children being so far away with strangers.

"Stay with me," Blaine said, seeing her distress, "there's more."

Penelope made an effort to control her emotions. "I'm ready. Please continue."

"Your children will come back to you. I promise, but not for 67 days. At that time, as he was meant to, Levi Burke will die from a heart attack."

Penelope's hand flew to her mouth to cover a brief gasp; however she found she felt no despair at this news.

"Only then will you be able to collect your children and bring them home."

"But where will we go?" Chloe asked. The men here believe we are dead."

"I was coming to that. For the next 67 days, you must stay out of sight. That's why Timothy believes you should come home with me, to the year 2017. You will still be at the manor, just in a different time. When the time and circumstances are right, you will be brought back here to your own time to live out your lives as you were meant to."

Both women were silent, pondering the things they had heard. After a nod from Chloe, Penelope said, "We trust you, Mr. Duncan. We shall do as you ask."

Blaine took them both by the hand and said into the darkness, "Timothy, I think we're ready."

A moment later they found themselves in the year 2017, though it was difficult to be sure until they made their way out of the trees and walked back through the cemetery and toward the house.

Chloe clung to Penelope as they made their way. She looked frightened, but determined to take whatever steps were necessary to be near to and watch over Penelope. It was still night, nearly 1 a.m., but the moon was full as it had been in the past.

"So many graves," Penelope said, "and the manor looks, different."

In the distance you could see the lights of the town of Machias as well as lights from the distant harbor.

"We are really in the future," Penelope breathed out in awe.

"Yes," Blaine smiled. "And I will show you many things, but first, I think we all need some sleep."

They were all exhausted, both physically and emotionally, yet the idea of sleep seemed like an impossibility to Penelope. There was so much to see and learn. Sleep seemed like a waste of precious time. However, she kept this thought to herself.

Blaine led them in the front entry and eventually to the second floor, but progress was slow. Penelope wanted to stop and look at all the changes to her home along the way. On the second floor he led them to the bathroom first to show them how everything worked and where they could find linen. Both women were slightly embarrassed but grateful. Next he brought them to the second suite. It had been Penelope's room in the past.

"There is a third room just across the hall if you don't want to share," he offered, but both women agreed that, at least for tonight, one room would be sufficient.

"I'll bring you some clothing. You're both about Christina's size. I'll be back in a moment."

He rummaged through Christina's wardrobe which he had refused to get rid of. He gathered two of her most conservative nightgowns, some floor length peasant skirts and appropriate tops. He thought that her underwear would probably seem far too skimpy for women of the 1600s, but added them anyway, leaving it to them to figure out. He brought the clothing to their room and knocked on the door.

"These are much different than what you're used to wearing,

I'm sure, but they're clean and it's what women wear these days. We can look through the rest of the clothing tomorrow."

"Thank you, Mr. Duncan. I'm sure this will be fine."

"You know," Blaine said, "you don't have to call me Mr. Duncan. Blaine is fine. May I call you Penelope?"

"Is that customary in this time period?" she asked.

"Yes. I guess things aren't as formal these days as they were in your time."

"Very well, then, Blaine. I shall try to blend in."

"Good. Well, good night then. I'll just be down the hall if you need anything. Get some rest. I have a surprise for you tomorrow."

It wasn't until Blaine returned to his room that he notice the paintings were back. He stood staring with relief at each one. Some of them had changed, but they were there. That meant the journal should also exist once again. That, too, was a relief because it meant he and Jack were friends once more.

He looked up and said softly, "Nice going, Timothy." Though he should have been exhausted both mentally and physically, he could not sleep. His mind danced wildly from one impossible event to the next as they had unfolded in the last twenty-four hours. Beginning in one timeline, he had been whisked back through the years by centuries. Next, he had been yanked back to the present, only to find that the original time-line had been changed. As if all that weren't enough to wreak havoc in any rational mind, he then found himself teaming up with an immortal who called himself a timekeeper. It seemed their new mission, his and this timekeeper's, was to go back yet again to change the incorrect timeline by bringing two women from the past into the present. And the craziest part of all—they weren't done yet.

As he lay in his bed alone in the master suite of this quiet house, he considered, just for a moment, that perhaps none of this had really happened. What if Christina's death had simply been too much for him? What if his overwhelming grief had driven him to delusions? What if this house which held the air of generations of human drama simply played to his growing madness, weaving tales of time travel in his mind?

No, that couldn't be true. Even insanity couldn't produce such an intricate tale. He looked to the paintings once again which hung around the room, clearly visible in the moonlight. They were all there, and he was still in every one.

Slowly he pushed the idea of insanity away, letting the wild visions in his mind calm themselves until he was finally able to sleep.

CHAPTER 17

When Blaine awoke the next morning his head was clear and he felt rested. There had been no nightmares of being burned alive, nor any waking visions of tortured souls who had been murdered by unjust men. The timeline, though slightly different from its original detail, had successfully been restored. At least, so far. This was a relief in many ways for Blaine. Not only were Penelope and Chloe safe, and hopefully, he and Jack were once again friends, but equally important to Blaine, it seemed the future was apparently NOT written in stone. Apparently the timekeeper and even Blaine, with the timekeeper's help, were able to make changes when necessary. This brought a whole new sense of relief to Blaine and gave him at least a small feeling of control over his own life.

As Timothy had said, Blaine was given the next day to live over. This was the day he would meet Melissa Sturgis, and now,

Penelope would meet her as well. What a perfect way to spend her first day in his time.

In spite of the day's string of terror-filled events and their eventual consequences, which brought the two women to the very doorstep of death, and maybe because of those events, Penelope and Chloe found both the distance in time, coupled with complete emotional exhaustion, sent them both into a deep and restful sleep. When they awoke the next morning, and once they had gathered their minds around the idea that they were now in the year 2017, they felt surprisingly safe and calm. The only tangible evidence of what had nearly occurred last night was the dresses they had worn. Burns could be found around the hem of each dress, and from the scorched dresses, the acrid scent of smoke wafted through the room.

Chloe tucked the scorched dresses away in the wardrobe. Each took turns freshening up in the wonderfully modern bathroom, and then they examined the clothing Blaine had brought them last night. They found it to be woefully immodest, and in the case of the undergarments, a bit confusing. Nevertheless, in deference to Blaine and his generous hospitality and timely rescue, they persevered until they believed they had mastered their new attire.

From the window of their room, Penelope eagerly took in her first daylight view of the year 2017. The cemetery, as she had noticed even under the cover of dark the previous night, held considerably more graves; however, from the vantage point of this room at least, there were few other differences. Of course, she knew the minute she left this room there would be differences she couldn't even begin to imagine.

Blaine was first downstairs. He decided breakfast was the first order of business. He brewed a pot of coffee, poured himself a cup, and was working on scrambled eggs and bacon when Chloe and Penelope entered the kitchen. Both women looked uncomfortable in the clothing he'd brought them the night before.

"Good morning, Mr... Blaine," Penelope corrected herself. "I trust you slept well?"

Blaine could see how *exposed* they both felt in their modern clothes. "You both look beautiful this morning," he said, trying to put them at ease. "Did you sleep well?"

"Yes, Sir," Chloe said, shyly.

"Let's get something straight," Blaine said in his kindest voice. "Both of you are my guests here. I want you to feel comfortable. There is no need to call me 'Sir'. Blaine will do just fine. Consider my home your home. It was yours first, after all."

"Thank you, Blaine," Chloe said with a sweet smile.

"Have you no servants to prepare your meals?" Penelope asked.

"Nope. I do it all myself. Of course, Christina helped with everything before, well, you know. Now it's just me. But if you want to set the table, the dishes are in that cupboard."

Chloe immediately moved to handle the task. Blaine rounded out the bacon and eggs with some fresh sliced cantaloupe and orange juice. Both women were fascinated as he explained the workings of the gas range and the electric refrigerator and lights.

"What a marvelous time you live in," Penelope said, "such wonders."

"I guess we take things for granted sometimes. It's all what you're used to, I suppose."

While they ate, Penelope reminded Blaine that he had said he had a surprise for her today. She smiled like an anxious child and it touched Blaine's heart. She was like Christina in so many ways.

"Indeed I did. You see, because we, Timothy and I, had to go back and change what happened yesterday, I actually get to live this day for a second time. Because of that, I know some of what will happen today."

Penelope listens intently, waiting for the surprise.

"I don't want to tell you too much about your future, but I will tell you this. One day, your son Alex will marry and have at least one child, a son. That son, in turn will have children, and so on. One of your great, great grandchildren, several generations from your time, will be here today. Her name is Melissa Sturgis and she is a direct descendent from Alex."

Penelope's eyes widened, then a smile spread slowly. "But, how, I mean, will she know who I am?"

"No. I met her as I was walking on the cliffs. She said she was writing a history of her family tree and had wanted to come here to see the original Burke family home. We just happened to meet. She doesn't know me and she won't know you. We can tell her you're my cousins, just visiting for a while. Would you like to meet her?"

Penelope was speechless for a moment.

"She looks a lot like you, Penelope," Blaine added, as a bit of encouragement.

Penelope needed no encouragement. "How wonderful that would be! Imagine, meeting my own great-granddaughter. How I wish Alex could be here for this extraordinary opportunity." She was absolutely beaming with anticipation. "Of course, I realize I must conceal my true identity," she was saying to no one in particular. "Perhaps we may learn something about her."

"Well, we won't meet her until this afternoon, so I think we should take care of a few things before then."

When they had finished eating, Blaine got to his feet and began clearing away the breakfast dishes. Chloe and Penelope joined him. Once again, they were fascinated by the workings of the automatic dishwasher. Once breakfast had been cleaned up, Blaine invited them to join him upstairs.

"We need to get you both set up with some appropriate clothing for your stay here. Please keep in mind that we had only begun renovations on the house when she died. The master suite has not yet been done, so things look a little skimpy in there."

He had them wait in the hall as he quickly went in alone and removed the paintings from the wall and stood them against the baseboard, facing away from view. "I don't believe it's a good idea for you to see the paintings you will make ahead of time," he explained. "We don't want anything else to change the timeline. Better to be cautious."

Blaine left the women to explore clothing options at their leisure, only taking a few minutes to show them where everything was. Chloe first noticed the wedding photo on the nightstand.

"Is this your wife?" she asked.

"Yes."

"A remarkable representation," she marveled.

"That's because it isn't a painting," Blaine said, realizing they had never seen photography before. "It's called a photograph. I don't think I can explain exactly how it works, so let's just call it 300 years of progress and leave it at that."

When the women had finished selecting their clothing and a few pairs of shoes, Blaine showed them the third bedroom, once again offering it to Chloe if she wanted. This time she accepted. Once clothing had been issued and freshening up had been done, Blaine barely mentioned the idea of exploring outside before they each rushed to the front door. He felt like he was taking excited children to Disneyland for the first time. He hadn't smiled this much in many months. Their excitement was contagious.

He grabbed the keys to the truck before leading them out of the house and toward the shop where the truck was parked.

"You asked me once what a car was," he said to Penelope. "Well, this is actually a truck a larger version of a car. Get in and I'll show you how it works."

He held the passenger door open and helped both women inside. Chloe took the rear seat and Penelope in the front. Blaine climbed in his side and put the key in the ignition.

"When I turn this key, it will create a spark in the engine which will ignite the fuel. We will then have a carriage that needs no horses."

He turned the key and the truck roared to life. Each women was holding her breath but they were excited as well. He backed the truck enough to get himself a space for turning around, then he brought them forward down the drive to the main road. There he stopped. The women began talking over each other in excitement.

"Extraordinary!"

"How does it work?"

"How fast does it go?"

"What makes it go backward or forward?"

... And many more questions. Blaine put it in reverse and backed them up to the shop where they had begun. He didn't try to answer their questions, but rather listened and smiled.

"I'm afraid that's as far as we go today. You'll need more time to be ready to see the town."

"The town?" Chloe asked.

"Yes. Machias. It's just beyond those trees down there."

Penelope sighed. "There was only a trading post there. How large is the town?"

"Oh, about a million three hundred thousand people, give or take a few thousand."

"Incredible! Why would so many people want to come to such a remote territory?" Penelope asked.

"Well, for one thing, Maine hasn't been a territory since the 1800s. It's now a state; one of fifty states in what is called the United States of America. And there are many cities with far more people in each one than here in Machias."

"You are correct, Blaine. I don't believe I'm quite ready to see that just yet."

Chloe had walked slightly ahead, giving an illusion of privacy to Blaine and Penelope; however she did not lead them back to the house. Instead she was moving toward the cemetery. Even from a distance she could see there were many graves, unlike the three small headstones she was accustomed to seeing. Blaine looked up to see where they were heading.

"May I see your wife's grave?" Penelope asked.

Blaine hesitated a moment. "Well, I haven't marked the grave yet, but I'll show you where she's buried. But, I don't think you should look at all the graves. There are some things we just shouldn't know ahead. Agreed?"

"Very well, but may I visit my babies?"

"Yes, of course you can."

They stopped at Christina's grave first. It was visible without a marker, but the grass was growing quickly. Blaine knew he would have to do something soon.

"May I ask," Penelope said, "why you have not yet marked your wife's grave?"

Blaine shoved his hands in his pockets and looked away. "I

don't know. I guess because I'm afraid that taking that final step would be like saying, 'I'm done with you. You are passed and gone and we are passed and gone too.' Does that sound crazy?"

Penelope's heart filled with compassion. She took a few steps to the graves of her babies. Kneeling down, she touched a kiss to the first from her fingertips, then to each grave as he had seen her do in her own time. "Mr. Duncan," she began, forgetting the less formal address, "we are not diminished by the brevity of our lives, nor are we made less by the passage of time, but shall remain always as we were, no less, and forever."

Her words did more than touch him. They poured into his heart. It was true. Christina could never be made less to him simply because she had died and some time had passed. Nothing would ever change the love he held for her in his heart. Penelope's words were beyond wisdom of the moment, but were universally and eternally true, and that truth was a thing of beauty. He was grateful.

CHAPTER 18

When the time came to walk out on the cliffs to meet Melissa Sturgis, Chloe chose to remain at the house to give Blaine and Penelope some time alone.

"What shall I say to her?" Penelope wondered aloud.

"Well, I would strongly suggest you don't give her your real name, for starters. Do you have a name you can use?"

Penelope thought for a moment. "I've always rather liked the name Anna. I think I shall be Anna Hollingsworth." She looked at Blaine for approval.

"Okay, Anna. You are my cousin from New York. What about Chloe?"

"She shall be my traveling companion. Will that do?"

"I guess we'll find out," Blaine said, pointing ahead, "there she is."

The young woman looked their way as they approached.

"I'm sorry. I hope I'm not trespassing," she said, just as she had before.

This time it was Penelope who stood stunned. It was like looking in a mirror at herself except the young woman's hair was much shorter.

"Ma'am, are you all right?"

"Yes, yes. I just thought you were someone else."

Blaine marveled at how the dialogue was, so far, identical except it was Penelope instead of him saying the words.

"My name is Melissa Sturgis. I wasn't sure where the property boundaries lay, but I wanted to see the place. I hope I didn't trespass?"

Blaine spoke while Penelope gathered herself. "No, you're fine."

"Good. You see, I've been making a record of my family history, and several generations back, my great-grandmother, Penelope Burke lived in that house. I'm a direct descendent of her son, Alex Burke. I've been told that I look something like her from an old painting."

Penelope had not spoken, but was smiling sweetly.

"I'm Blaine Duncan, the current owner, and this is my cousin Anna Hollingsworth, visiting from New York."

Melissa turned to Penelope for her first real look at her. "My goodness," she said, "I believe I look more like you than my great-grandmother. How strange is that?"

"I'm so pleased to meet you," Penelope said, taking Melissa's hand in hers. Without letting go, she turned to Blaine and said, "Perhaps we should invite her in to see the house."

Blaine couldn't contain his smile. "My thoughts, exactly; right this way, ladies."

"Oh, this is very kind of you," Melissa said excitedly. "I never expected I would get to go inside. May I take pictures? They would be wonderful to have in my book."

Penelope didn't understand the question so she looked to Blaine for a response.

"Sure," Blaine answered, "but I must warn you, my wife and I have only recently begun renovation. Much of the house is unfinished inside."

"I hope your wife doesn't mind," Melissa said.

"She passed away last year. It will just be Anna and her traveling companion, Chloe, and I."

"Oh, I'm sorry Mr. Duncan. I didn't realize."

"No harm done," Penelope offered. "I hope you enjoy the tour."

Penelope suddenly wished they had informed Chloe of the name change and status before they had left the house. She would just have to hope she could have a brief word with her before there was a blunder. Blaine was having similar thoughts as they entered the house.

Penelope left them briefly in the entry saying she was going to inform Chloe they had a guest. As Penelope hurried up the stairs, Blaine showed Melissa the library and parlor on the main floor. They were just about to look into the still vacant dining room when Penelope and Chloe came downstairs. Penelope made a quick introduction and the two women greeted each other politely.

"If it wouldn't be too much trouble," Melissa asked, "may I get a picture of the three of you in front of the staircase?"

Penelope and Chloe both looked at Blaine for an explanation, but didn't want to ask any questions that might give them away.

"I think that's a great idea," Blaine said, "on one condition. I'd like you to take a second picture with my old Polaroid. I collect them," he lied. He disappeared into the library for the one Polaroid he did own. It had actually belonged to Christina and it had only a few shots left in it.

The three of them stood together for Melissa's pictures. Penelope and Chloe had no idea what was happening but they smiled when instructed, heard a buzz and a click sound from the object in Melissa's hands, and then they were apparently finished. Both women failed to see the purpose in such a ritual, but they said nothing.

Then Blaine took Melissa's place, asking Anna and Melissa to stand together while he took a photo with the Polaroid. Finally, he asked Melissa to take one final Polaroid of him and Anna together. Blaine took both prints and put them into his shirt pocket as they completed the tour. When they reached the master suite, he heard Melissa say to Anna the same words she had said to him the day before.

"So this is where my great-grandmother slept."

"I believe it was customary in those days for the lady of the house to have her own bedchamber. Perhaps your great-grandmother slept in the adjoining room."

That was a much better answer than his fumbling words, Blaine thought to himself. He couldn't help but notice how lovingly Penelope spoke to Melissa. He hoped it wasn't too obvious to Melissa as well.

When the tour was complete and the four of them stood once again in the entry, Penelope said, "Tell us about yourself, dear. Are you married? Do you have a family?"

"I am recently married," she said. We have no children yet."

"And you have a happy life with your new husband, I trust?"

Melissa seemed uncomfortable by the personal nature of the question, but answered, "Yes, we're very happy." Then she added, "I really must be going. I have an early flight tomorrow and I need to organize today's photos and record. Thank you all so much for your hospitality. This will be the crowning jewel of my book."

"It was a pure delight having you here," Penelope said. "Your ancestors would be proud, I'm sure."

As Melissa stepped through the door, Penelope called after her, "Be well, Melissa. Goodbye."

When the door closed behind her, Penelope turned to Blaine. "I have just experienced what is not possible, and yet it has happened. It was marvelous. And I have you to thank. May I embrace you, Mr. Duncan?"

Blaine was surprised but pleased by her request. He opened his arms to her and she rushed in.

"Thank you for this gift you have given me. Thank you for our lives and this extraordinary journey on which we have embarked. You can't possibly realize what you have done for me."

"You're welcome," Blaine said, not sure what else to say.

Penelope backed out of his embrace. "Forgive me, Mr. Duncan. I'm afraid I am overcome with emotion and not in complete control of myself. I pray I have not overstepped."

"It's quite all right," Blaine said. "I'm glad you're happy. And remember, you can call me Blaine."

"I shall work on that," she smiled. "Remember, I may be in the modern time, but I am still an old-fashioned woman. Some things just don't come easy. I believe I shall retire to my room for a rest, if that's alright."

"Of course, but before you go, I have something to show you."

He fished in his shirt pocket for the now developed pictures and handed them to Penelope. Her eyes widened as she saw herself and her great-granddaughter standing side-by-side in one photo and herself and Blaine in the other.

"Remarkable! It's like magic. What a wondrous time this is where all manner of impossibilities are possible."

"They're yours," Blaine said. "To help you remember."

She pressed the photos to her heart and hurried up the stairs to her room.

CHAPTER 19

Over the next few days Blaine considered calling Jack, but he hesitated for fear things might not still be the same between them. He decided it would be best if he waited for Jack to call or show up. That way, he would know for sure. Meanwhile, the three of them explored some of the changes to the manor. Both Penelope and Chloe learned how to use the gas range and oven, the dishwasher and the washer and dryer. Blaine decided that the television and online computer would provide them with too much information about today's world, so did not explain these devices to them.

In the evenings, they would sit and discuss how they would return to the manor of their time when 67 days had passed. None of the three could figure out a way to do that without looking as though they had returned from the dead. All of the men of their time had witnessed their deaths by fire.

This had Penelope and Chloe very concerned. What if she couldn't return with a suitable explanation? What if she could not bring her children home? Furthermore, had Levi Burke told the children she was dead, or worse, had he told them she was a witch?

Blaine suggested to them that Timothy may have already worked that out, but, in truth, he wasn't sure of that.

On the morning of the fourth day, May 24th, shortly after breakfast, Jack Rush drove up to the manor.

Alex sat on one of the three small beds in the crowded boarding room. He had been given the option of his own room away from the girls, but he would not leave his sisters alone.

"Why can't we go home?" Ingrid asked sadly.

Alex gathered her to his side on the bed, but said nothing.

"Father says Mother is too ill. We must stay until she is well again." Miriam said.

Alex replied in angry tones. "Father is a liar. We all saw Mother the night before he brought us here. She was not ill. And if she were ill, she would not want us to leave her. Something else is wrong."

"I want to go home," Ingrid whined. "I miss Mother."

"We will go home," Alex assured her. "I promise. Just give me some time to think about this."

Esther Reese poked her head into the children's room. She had been kind to them and Alex knew she meant well, but he refused to warm to her. It felt like doing so would be like betraying his mother.

"It's late children. You should all be sleeping," she said kindly. "Perhaps tomorrow your father will stop in to see you."

It was meant as an encouragement; however, Alex had no wish to see his father unless he was preparing to take them home. Beyond that, his father held no place of value in Alex's life. He knew also that he was simply "the man who brought gifts" to the girls. He had never made any worthy attempt to bond with his children. Alex's biggest frustration was that he had not realized this earlier. He loathed the memory of desiring his father's love and approval for so many years. That would never again be the case.

He tucked the girls in, one by one, promising them once again that he would get them home.

Jack came around to the kitchen door as he always did. Blaine was there to meet him. Thankfully, Jack spoke first when Blaine opened the door.

"Hey, Blaine. How have you been? You haven't called all week. I was afraid something was wrong."

That sounded like the Jack he knew. Blaine felt relief.

"C'mon in, Jack. It's been a rather interesting week. There's someone I want you to meet, actually, two people. They're in the parlor."

Jack followed Blaine through the house to the parlor. When they entered, Jack saw two women sitting and conversing quietly. At first nothing seemed unusual until the one woman whose back had been turned to Jack turned his way. Jack's jaw dropped as Blaine introduced them.

"May I introduce Penelope Burke and her companion, Chloe." Blaine suddenly realized he didn't know Chloe's last name and he inquired of her.

"Dunnigan," Chloe said. "Chloe Dunnigan."

Jack was barely paying attention to this new piece of information. He was looking back and forth between Penelope and Blaine, waiting for an explanation.

"You'd better sit down, Jack. We've got quite a story to tell you."

Though Jack looked stunned, it wasn't for the reasons Blaine thought. He was a bit awestruck at seeing Penelope Burke face-to-face, but he was not surprised she was there. As he settled himself next to Blaine on the second sofa facing the women he said, "I believe I already know the story. I just didn't know it had happened already."

The other three sat with confused expressions.

"What do you mean you already know?" Blaine asked.

"I told you before, Blaine, but you didn't want to hear it. It's the journal. I wanted to warn you... keep you safe... all of you. But you wouldn't let me show you."

Chloe and Penelope were still confused, but Blaine was beginning to understand. Timothy had told him the women would remember all of this when they returned to their own time. He had also said there would be some minor changes like the paintings, but nothing that would have a significant impact on the timeline. Apparently, Penelope's journal would be changed to include recent events. For Jack, however, it was still the same journal he'd found as a boy. To him, it had included these events all along.

"Unbelievable," Blaine said, more to himself than the others. He looked at Jack and nodded his understanding.

Jack smiled. "That's why I had to come today. I was worried about what you might be facing on your next trip. Even though you said you didn't want to know, I decided I had to tell you anyway. It seems I was a bit late, though. I'm glad to see you all made it back safely."

It seemed that Blaine alone would know how it was when the timeline was changed by Penelope's and Chloe's deaths. Even Penelope's journal could not tell of her hauntings at Burkeshire Manor over the past 300 years, or the loss of Blaine's friendship with Jack, or the tormented and lonely man Blaine would have been, never having traveled back through time. None of them would know any of this except Blaine, and, of course, the timekeeper. He knew it was better that way.

Blaine encouraged Jack to bring the women up to speed on the journal, then sat back and listened as Jack told the story of how he had found the journal as a boy and had been waiting all these years for Blaine to come to Machias and purchase the manor. Blaine stopped him short of revealing the contents of the journal except for the most general information.

When Jack had finished, Blaine said, "Jack has been the only one I could talk to about this, my travels through time, the paintings, and how crazy it all was. Because of the journal, Jack knew I wasn't crazy. He's been a great friend. I don't know how I would have coped with all this if he hadn't been here to keep it all in perspective."

"So, there you have it ladies. We now know all about each other," Jack said. "I must say, it's a pleasure."

"Excuse me, Mr. Rush," Penelope said, "It seems you've had the advantage. You are the only one who has read my journal. Tell me, does it mention in the journal how I shall return to our time without the men believing we have returned from the dead?"

It was a good question. All three turned to Jack, waiting for his answer.

I'm afraid I can't recall an explanation for that situation. I would be happy to search for any clues. Blaine, don't you have any ideas about that?"

"Sorry. I have been trying to figure that out, but I've got nothing."

"Well, I know this," Jack said, "it must have worked out because you did return home and things went well. I guess we'll just have to have some faith things will go as they're supposed to."

Everyone was quietly contemplative. Jack could feel the heaviness in the room. He felt the need to lift the mood. "Look, this is my only day off this week. What do you say we all run down to the harbor, pick up some seafood and take a little cruise on the bay?"

Penelope and Chloe turned to Blaine awaiting a translation.

"Jack means he would like us to drive down to the harbor, buy some lunch and take it on a boat we can take out on the water."

"Didn't I say that?" Jack said.

Everyone chuckled softly.

"It sounds lovely," Penelope said.

Chloe chimed in. "I have never done anything like that. It sounds wonderful."

Jack looked at Chloe's wide-eyed expression as she considered the pending adventure. He was a bit surprised to feel a mild attraction to her childlike innocence and softly feminine appeal.

"Great," Blaine said. "Why don't the two of you go on upstairs and put on some pants and maybe some warm sweaters. It's a little cool on the water. I'll grab a couple of lap blankets."

"I'll call the harbor and reserve a boat. There should be plenty available this early in the season," Jack said.

In twenty minutes, everyone was ready to go. Penelope and Chloe were a bit uncomfortable wearing what they considered to be trousers; however they were a little less uncomfortable than they had been a few days ago.

They decided to take Jack's Range Rover for better seating. This would be the first time Chloe and Penelope had been able to travel beyond the end of the driveway. It was difficult to contain their excitement.

"Will there be many people in the harbor?" Chloe asked.

"Not as many as in town, but some." Blaine answered. "But once we get out on the water, it'll just be the four of us."

Both Chloe and Penelope were relieved. As much as they were curious to see the population of the present day, they felt it was an experience best taken in small doses. The two women watched in awe as they turned on to the main road, traveling faster than any carriage could go. They passed many homes of varying sizes and styles, with beautiful lawns. Many displayed design work imitating seagoing vessels. There were many cars, both on the road and standing outside of homes. It seemed that everyone owned at least one. The road itself was a fascination as well, so smooth and firm.

They drove from the high point of the manor downward, weaving around many curves as they made their way to the harbor. As the harbor came into view, they saw several docks to which many boats were tethered. However, it seemed these boats were as far advanced as a car was to a carriage. Sleek ribbons of white, blue, red and a few other colors lined each dock.

As they got closer they could see several buildings, some appeared to be maintenance buildings, others apparently sold seagoing supplies, and still others seemed to cater to visitors.

"That's where we're going," Jack said, pointing a short distance ahead. "The Harbor Lights Restaurant; the best seafood on two coasts."

The women could see there were many cars parked there. They hoped the crowd would not be too large.

"I'm going to drop you and Blaine off here," he said to Penelope. "The two of you can order for all of us. Chloe and I will drive on down there to take care of the boat rental. Then we'll be back to pick you two up. Is everyone okay with that?"

The women were both so out of their element, it didn't seem to matter who went with who. "I suppose so," Penelope said.

"You okay with that Chloe?" Jack asked.

Chloe had been a servant most of her life. Being asked for her opinion or approval was not something she was used to.

"Yes, Mr. Rush. As you wish."

"Please," Blaine said again, "it's Blaine and Jack. No Mister. People will think we're tyrants if you call us that."

Not wanting to stand out unnecessarily, Chloe said, "Very well then, Jack. It is clear to us that you are not tyrants. We surely do not want to misrepresent your character in public."

"Much better," Jack said as he pulled up in front of the restaurant. "Chloe and I will swing by the harbor market and pick up some beverages for the trip. We'll probably get all that done by the time the food is ready. Don't forget to order some crab, and some loaves of that good garlic bread."

Blaine and Penelope stepped out of the vehicle and Jack and Chloe moved on. Blaine took Penelope by the hand and she did not object.

"Come on," he said "let's go inside."

In spite of the many vehicles parked outside, the restaurant was nearly empty, at least as far as they could see into the room. A young woman stepped up to greet them and offered to seat them at a table. Blaine explained, however, that they wanted meals to go. The two of them were given menus to look at but Penelope left the choices to Blaine. He selected two seafood platters for a variety of taste, a crab dinner and a lobster dinner.

"Don't forget the bread loaves," Penelope whispered.

"Oh, yes, and two loaves of garlic bread," he added.

The waitress smiled at the quantity of food, Blaine noticed.

"We're ordering for four. We're taking dinner out on the bay," Blaine explained. "It will be the first time for the two ladies."

"Well, I hope you have a wonderful time," she said to Penelope.

"I'm sure we shall," Penelope answered in pure lady's fashion.

Blaine couldn't help but smile at her always proper speech. He found it charming, though he was sure the waitress found it a bit odd, at the very least.

While Penelope and Blaine waited for dinner, Jack and Chloe had checked in at the harbor office and filled out the necessary paperwork, paid for the day cruiser and were now on their way to the harbor market for drinks.

"It's all very exciting, eating dinner on a boat out on the water, don't you think?" Chloe was out of her element, both in time and socially, but she seemed to be adapting rapidly. "Do you do this sort of thing often?"

"Only when I have a special guest to share it with." Jack was referring to the special circumstances of the two time traveling women, but he realized that to Chloe it probably sounded like he was flattering her. She blushed, smiled, and said nothing.

They had reached the market. Jack selected several options. When they reached the checkout stand they had bottles of flavored teas, sodas, a six-pack of Heineken and some bottled water. He purposely kept the alcohol to a minimum as they would be boating and, well, he was a cop after all.

When they returned to the restaurant Blaine stepped out and motioned for Jack to give him a hand. Penelope slid into the back seat with Chloe while Jack and Blaine loaded package after package of wrapped food onto their laps, finally taking the last of it up front while they drove down to park near the docks. The delicious aromas filled the vehicle and everyone agreed dinner would be first on the agenda once they left the harbor.

Jack had chosen a 21-foot Bayliner Caprice Sport. It was comfortable for eight, but quite roomy for four. They quickly loaded the food, blankets and themselves into the boat and Jack fired her up and expertly maneuvered them out of the harbor.

The day was hovering around 70°. Not too hot, and a comfortable breeze as they sped through the water to the outer southwest portion of the bay. Penelope and Chloe both grasped the railing with white knuckles; however the smiles never left their faces. Jack brought the boat to rest below the cliffs of the manor. Its windows glistened in the midday sun, its features barely distinguishable from its former glory at this distance.

Even Blaine noticed the way it bore a strange resemblance to its early days. Only he and the women could appreciate the impact of that.

Penelope tried to find the words to express what she was feeling. "If I should die in my sleep this night, I shall have experienced more wonder, kindness and beauty than any woman could hope to imagine in a lifetime."

Blaine and Jack looked at each other briefly, but both turned away quickly so as not to reveal the depth of emotion each felt at her words.

"Well, I don't know about you guys, but I'm starving. How about we get going on those dinners," Blaine said.

For the next three hours everyone enjoyed good food, pleasant and frequently entertaining conversation and long periods of contented silence as Jack took them skillfully across the waters opening up an ever changing range of scenery for their enjoyment.

Thankfully, no one experienced seasickness, however, the ladies' cheeks and noses had begun to turn a bit pink from the long exposure to the sun off the water.

Noticing this, Jack said, "I think we should probably call it a day and bring the boat back into shore. I don't want to have to treat sunburns at the end of an otherwise perfect day."

Everyone agreed it had been a long day in the sun and no one's skin had been tempered since winter had been upon them. Burning would be too easy this early in the year.

When the charter had been re-secured in the harbor and

the four of them were on their way back to the manor, each rode in near silence with only a few words passing among them. Everyone was content and a bit drowsy from the fresh air and good food. It had been an intoxicating day in so many ways, one that would be remembered for a very long time.

CHAPTER 20

That evening when everyone had retired to their rooms, Chloe lay in bed thinking of the wonderful day they had enjoyed, and more particularly about Jack Rush. As a servant, she realized she had always held very low expectations for herself where matters of the heart were concerned. It was not uncommon for a woman such as herself to be in service to others for her entire life. This thought was no more disturbing to her than a life-long career would be to you or me in the present day, but the difference was that for women like Chloe, it often meant never marrying, never having children, or never having your own home where you could privately enjoy your own family. If such a woman was fortunate, as Chloe believed she had been, she would find herself in the service of a fine family with a loving home in which she was considered a part.

Chloe loved Penelope and loved the children as her own.

She had always been treated very well and quite fairly in the many years of service she had given the Burke family. But this night, as she lay in her bed thinking, she began to wonder if there might be more for her.

Jack Rush had been more than simply kind to her today. He had treated her as an equal, as though he had never even considered treating her any other way. Furthermore, she believed he was a bit enchanted by her as she had been by him. Certainly a fine gentleman such as himself would never pursue a servant in any serious way, but she did allow herself a few moments to indulge in such a fantasy.

Chloe was not the only one indulging in such fantasies that night. Jack sat in front of the TV watching one of his favorite old movies with John Wayne. To be accurate, he was not actually paying much attention to the movie. His mind had wandered to the events of the day. He was feeling rather like all was well in the world at that moment. Blaine had, indeed, come to Machias to buy the manor. He had found the paintings as the journal had said he would, and begun his travels through time. They had successfully escaped Levi Burke's murderous plans and were all safely in the present day for the time being. But, what really occupied the majority of his thoughts tonight was Chloe Dunnigan. Even sitting alone in his house, he was a little embarrassed at how the thought of her sent a flurry of butterflies through him.

Not once in the two years since Nancy had died had he been even remotely attracted to another woman. Chloe was so pure and delicate, like a porcelain doll, but so soft in nature that one would almost believe she would break apart like the tiny seed heads of a dandelion if you grasped her too firmly.

It did not escape him that these feelings were dangerous. He knew she would only be here for now fewer than 67 more days. She did not belong in his world any more than he belonged in hers. He knew he should resist these feelings for both their sakes. They would only bring unhappiness in the end. Yet, as he sat there tonight, he continued to imagine scenarios that could never be.

As Jack had told everyone that morning, he wouldn't have another day off for almost a week, but as soon as his shifts were done, he would make his way to the manor, often calling ahead to say he was bringing dinner for everyone. Once, it was Chinese, once it was Mexican, and one night it was Pizza. "You can't come to the 21st century and not experience pizza and beer," he had said. "That's just wrong."

As they all sat around the kitchen table eating pizza and drinking beer that night, they listened first to Jack and then to Blaine as they summarized the stories of their lives.

Jack described how his parents had come to Machias just after they were married. He was born here and had been here all his life. He told how he was a second generation cop, (then had to explain the word cop). He told how he and Nancy had known each other since grade school and had married shortly after graduation. For reasons they never knew, they were unable to have children, but they lived happily together for more than twenty years. Then she got sick. She died less than a year after she was diagnosed with cancer. Since then, it had just been work. "The only thing I really had to look forward to at that point was the day Blaine would come to Machias and buy the manor as the journal had said he would. You can imagine how excited I was when he showed up." He looked at Chloe. "It's been nothing but good since then."

"How about you, Blaine?" Penelope asked. "Tell us your story."

"Well, I was born in New York City, one of the largest cities in the country. I never liked the city; too many people, too much of everything, really. My father was the CEO of Duncan and Werther Pharmaceuticals, but the real money came from government research contracts. All my life I heard that money and power were the way to success. I never believed that. I always thought success was something that happened on a more personal level. Hence, my parents and I don't speak often. I haven't even told them Christina died.

As soon as I was old enough I left New York and moved to Manhattan, where I met Christina. She was a pastry chef at a restaurant I liked. One day I had an especially delicious desert at this restaurant and I asked the waiter if I could meet the man who had made it. They brought me Christina. There was no going back from there. We dated for about a year and were married. She loved making pastries, but hated working in the restaurant. She wanted her own place. As we talked about it over time, the discussion moved to the idea of a bed and breakfast. We began looking for something out of the city. One day, we heard about this place. It only took seeing it once and we were hooked. She loved it. We both did. I'm just sorry she never got to see her plans completed."

"We're all sorry," Chloe said. "I'm sure she was a wonderful woman."

"I'm certain she is proud of you for your courage and kindness to me and Chloe," Penelope added. "I know I would be."

"Would you ladies like to share some stories?" Jack asked.

"I think not," Penelope answered quickly, "perhaps another time."

"Okay, then. If not stories, I suggest we dance."

"Dance?" Blaine said. "How many beers have you had, Jack?"

"But we have no music," Chloe said.

"Fear not, ladies. Follow me."

Jack led everyone to the great room and asked them to wait. "I'll be right back."

Chloe was all smiles. Blaine and Penelope were mildly amused. A few minutes later Jack returned with his laptop.

"You have wifi, don't you Blaine?"

"Yeah," he said warily.

"Good. Just give me a minute." He opened the laptop, took a minute to log in then he called up the site he wanted. "Here we go," he announced, "ballroom music for the perfect evening at home."

The women were astonished at the sound of music coming from the flat box.

Jack turned to Chloe. "Would you care to waltz, my lady?"

"What a character," Blaine said. "Well, why not,. Penelope, would you do me the honor? I haven't done this in years," Blaine warned, "and I wasn't very good at it then. I'll try not to step on your toes too much."

Penelope smiled. "It has been years for me as well. I was barely eighteen the last time I danced."

Blaine took her in his arms, but not too close, as they waltzed to the music. Her husband may have tried to kill her recently, and they both knew he would die soon enough, but to Penelope, she was still a married woman and she was too much of a lady to forget that. Blaine respected her for that.

The inferior speakers on the laptop lent a tinny sound to the music, but the volume was sufficient to be heard around the large room. When the music changed, they changed partners for another round.

Chloe was almost beside herself with enjoyment. She had never been to a ball, and as far as she was concerned, this one was as grand as any.

For a while, all thoughts of lost loves, lost children, murderous husbands, and separations in time were put aside. In 300 years, Burkeshire Manor had never hosted a grand ball. Tonight was the first, and even if there were only four in attendance, it was indeed grand.

Nearly two hours later when all were exhausted, they

decided to call it a night. The women came away with only minor injuries to their toes, but everyone agreed it had been an excellent evening. Jack gathered up his laptop and Chloe walked him to the door. As they said goodnight, Jack hesitated.

"Chloe, I'm not sure what is appropriate for you, and Lord knows I've been out of the dating scene for a while. I guess what I'm trying to say is I would like to kiss you goodnight. Would that be okay with you?"

Chloe smiled that beautiful soft smile Jack loved. "I would like that very much, Jack." He leaned in to her turned up face and kissed her very softly on the lips. "Goodnight, Chloe. Thank you for dancing with me tonight." Then he turned and left before the desire to gather her in his arms overtook him.

Penelope and Blaine had gone to the kitchen to tidy up the mess they had left of pizza boxes and empty beer bottles.

"It was a lovely evening. I felt like a girl again. I am in awe at the contrast between my life here with you and the life I've led in my own time. Were it not for the children..." She left the rest of the thought unspoken.

Chloe came into the kitchen to help with the clean-up.

"We're nearly finished, Chloe. Why don't you go ahead upstairs. Goodnight, my dear friend. I do so hope you enjoyed the evening. Sleep well."

When Chloe had gone from the room, Blaine said, "I'm sorry your life has been so lonely. Levi didn't know what a lucky man he was. We're not so different, you and I. We've both been without the love we need. I realize that you are still a married woman right now, and I'm not trying to overstep my bounds. I'm just saying that maybe Christina was right. Maybe we can help each other. I know that being with you has certainly helped me, and I hope I can bring some happiness into your life, too."

Penelope looked into Blaine's eyes. "You really have no idea, do you? Even before I arrived here, but especially in these past several days, you have brought more hope and joy into my life than I had ever thought possible. I have never had what you and Christina had or what Jack and Nancy had. My marriage to Mr. Burke was arranged by my father. This marriage was my obligation to my family, nothing more. My children and my dear Chloe are all that I love."

The words came pouring out of her as if she had been waiting for years for someone to hear them. Blaine could see that she was already feeling embarrassed by these revelations. "Forgive me, Mr. Duncan. I'm afraid the alcohol has loosed my tongue. Perhaps we should say goodnight."

She turned and left the kitchen hurriedly, before he could say anymore. Blaine let her go. After the things she had just told him, he admired her even more for her courage and loyalty. She was a lady in every sense of the word. What a fool Levi Burke had been to take this remarkable woman for granted.

In spite of the late hour, all four of them, Blaine, Chloe, Penelope and Jack did not sleep easily that night. Each had their own thoughts and feelings to ponder as they lay in the darkness. Each was actively taking part in a most extraordinary happening. They each must remember that except for this brief number of days, they were truly separated by 300 years of time. That was not an obstacle easily overcome. Indeed, one they could never overcome on their own. It seemed that when all was said and done, it was entirely up to the timekeeper

CHAPTER 21

When morning came, Blaine went down to the kitchen to make some coffee. It was about 8:30. When it was ready, he poured himself a cup, drank it, and poured another. By 9:00, the women were still in their rooms.

They had all gone to bed late, and all had more than a few beers. He decided to let them sleep. Besides, he had an errand to run. He wanted to give Penelope something she was probably missing by now. He wrote a note saying he had to run to town for a while but would be back soon. He left it on the kitchen table.

As he rolled into town, the streets were quiet, except for the shopkeepers who were opening doors and setting out the usual merchandise on the sidewalks. Machias was a tourist town and a commercial fishing town. The two industries had built and sustained her for many years. On the tourist side, many people would come to capture the spectacular ocean views, some of them, artists like Penelope. For them, there were two or three shops in town which carried paints and canvases and other art supplies. Blaine pulled up in front of the nearest one.

Inside, a man who reminded Blaine a little of Mr. Rogers, listened to his request. "I have a friend who is visiting for a while. She is a painter, but is here without her supplies. (So far, all of this was true.) I thought I would pick up some things for her while she's here."

"If she came without supplies, I'm afraid the list could get a bit long," he said. "She will need canvas, oils, brushes, cleaners and probably an easel. Are you okay with that?"

"I'll tell you what," Blaine said. "I have another errand to run. Why don't you get everything together you think she'll need. I'll leave you my card and I'll be back in twenty minutes." Blaine slipped his credit card from his wallet and slid it across the counter to the Mr. Rogers lookalike. "Will this one work?"

The man looked at the name on the card. "You're Mr. Duncan, the man who bought the old manor. Yes, sir. This will work just fine."

"Good. I'll be back in twenty minutes."

His next stop was the music store. There, he shopped for a selection of music CD's from classical to jazz, soft rock and even some Motown. At the last minute, he threw in his personal favorite, Elvis. "I'll need a portable CD player to go with these. Something with good speakers," he told the clerk.

When he had finished at the music store, he returned for

the art supplies. Together with the store owner, they loaded everything into the back seat of the truck's cab, except the easel which Blaine laid carefully in the bed of the truck. He signed the charge slip and retrieved his card, thanking the shop owner for gathering all he needed.

"It was my pleasure, Mr. Duncan. Please let me know if there is anything else I can do for you."

Blaine supposed it was sometimes nice to not have to be concerned about money, especially when you wanted to do something nice for someone who really deserved it.

It was almost 10:30 when Blaine returned to the manor. Penelope and Chloe were in the library browsing some of the material Christina and Blaine had collected. Blaine called out to them as he entered by the kitchen. Penelope and Chloe met him there.

"I hope you both had a fine rest while I was gone. I had a few errands to run in town this morning."

"We are quite well, thank you," Penelope said. "May we be of assistance?"

"Actually, yes," Blaine said with a smile. "I believe there are a few items which may be of interest to you in the truck."

They both followed him out to the truck. Blaine opened the passenger door where a multitude of shopping bags covered the passenger seat and the seat behind it. Blaine began passing light weight bags to the women until their arms were full, then he picked up the box containing the CD player and two canvases from the back.

"Are those…" Penelope began.

"Look in the bags," Blaine said.

Penelope shifted her loaded arms until she was able to open one bag. Inside were brushes of various widths and textures. She looked up at Blaine, speechless.

"C'mon. Let's take everything inside. I've got something for you, too, Chloe."

They brought all the packages to the kitchen and spread them on the table. There were many bags filled with art supplies and Penelope went through them like she was unwrapping fine china.

"This is so kind of you, Blaine. I don't know what to say. Thank you sounds so inadequate."

"Just enjoy them. That's thanks enough. I'll have to go out to the truck to get the easel. But, before I do that, I have something for you Chloe."

Chloe's eyes lit up. "Something for me?"

Blaine took the CD player out of the box and selected a classical CD from those he had bought. "This is called a CD player and this is a CD. Each one of these holds an hour or so of music. Here, let me show you how it works."

He went on to show Chloe how she could either plug it in or use it on battery power, depending on where she wanted to listen. He showed her how to load the CD, control the volume, how to turn it on or off and a few other features. "Now you can listen to music any time you want, anywhere you want."

"You are too kind," she said, then, without warning, gave Blaine a fierce hug.

"You're welcome. I hope you enjoy the music I picked out. There are more CD's in the library. Some you may like, and some you might not. You'll just have to listen and decide."

They spent the next couple of hours getting Penelope's paints and supplies set up in her room near the window for the best light, just as she had done in her own time. The rest of the time was spent helping Chloe to test several CD's to determine which music she liked best. As it turned out, she was quite fond of the Elvis CD. Others she liked, aside from the classical, were Dean Martin, and, surprisingly, The Temptations.

When lunch time rolled around, Blaine could only get them away from their new treasures for a brief, light lunch of sandwiches, before they returned to their art and music.

"Well," Blaine mused to himself, "maybe I'm not the dazzling host I thought I was. It didn't take much for them to leave me behind."

He was glad they were happy. There wasn't really a lot to do around the house unless you were working on a project which is usually how he spent his days before the women arrived. He thought how the same must be true in their own time. Chloe, at least, had chores to attend to, but Penelope had servants for all that. Aside from her painting and time spent with her children, she really had nothing to do with her time. Every day would be the same. There were no other women to visit who didn't already live in the house. There was nowhere to go shopping except the trading post. There were no distractions of any kind. No wonder she had been so excited about Blaine's travels through time to visit her. She wasn't kidding when she said her life was predictable.

Suddenly Blaine knew why the timekeeper had done this, and for the first time, he could say without reservation, he was glad he did.

That afternoon while Blaine was in the still empty dining room sanding down the woodwork, Penelope came in and asked if she could speak with him privately for a few minutes.

"Sure, what can I do for you?" he asked with a smile.

"I'm afraid I must apologize," she began. "Last night in the kitchen, I said some things, or rather I told you some things that were not appropriate. It was wrong of me to say those things. I trust they will not be repeated."

Blaine thought a moment, and then he cupped Penelope's face in one of his hands so that they were looking at each other. "Were those things true?"

"That isn't the point…"

"That is exactly the point," Blaine challenged. "It may have been common practice in your day to have an arranged marriage, but not today, at least not in this country. You have spent all of these years with a man you don't love and who doesn't love you, and for what? Because he and your father made an agreement? All you did last night was admit to your own feelings about that. There's nothing to apologize for. That's what friends do—share their feelings with one another. We are friends, aren't we?"

Penelope could contain herself no longer. She fell into Blaine's arms weeping softly. "Indeed we are friends. I am more grateful to you than words can express."

"It's about time," Blaine said, holding her gently.

"I beg your pardon?"

"I was wondering what it would take for you to stop being the brave soldier and let your feelings come out. It's okay to admit you're sad and lonely. We both have been. You can trust me. I will always be here for you," and then he added, to lighten up the mood with a bit of humor, "or there for you."

Penelope smiled, then in spite of her tears. "I do trust you, Blaine. I knew the first time I saw you in the window that I need not fear you. I have looked forward to each of our visits with anxious anticipation, but I am afraid of things neither you nor I can control. Things like how I shall be able to return to my time and not be remembered for having died. What shall I say to my children concerning my absence? Even worse, what has Levi told them? I continue to fear these things and more, however, I do not doubt you or your friendship."

He wiped a remnant tear from her cheek. "I'm glad to hear that. As for the things you fear, I guess we'll just have to trust that Timothy is taking care of all that. So, how about I clean up in here, then you and I can go find something relatively tasty and nutritious for dinner, before Jack calls to say he's bringing take-out again."

"A splendid idea," Penelope said, looking much brighter than when she had walked in.

As they made their way to the kitchen a few minutes later, they could hear the sound of Elvis crooning "Are You Lonesome Tonight" as it drifted down the stairs.

Jack arrived about six and Chloe met him at the front door. She was excited to tell him of her new music box and Penelope's paints. Blaine and Penelope put the final touches on dinner while Jack and Chloe visited in the parlor.

Penelope was thinking to herself how strange it was that her personal maid was busy in the parlor with a suitor while she was in the kitchen preparing dinner. She had to smile at the contradiction. She had actually enjoyed preparing meals, tidying her room, doing laundry and dishes, and not just because it filled her time, but because she like doing these things for herself. Until her marriage to Levi Burke, she had not grown up with wealth. Hers was an average family where her mother labored in the home without the aid of servants. Her father worked as a supervisor for one of Levi's mills. The arranged marriage had been good for her family. Penelope thought to herself that perhaps she would do some cooking when she returned home. Mrs. Wilmington and Miss Millie would surely think she had gone mad. That thought made her smile as well.

Noticing the smiles, Blaine said, "You look happy. What are you smiling about?"

"Oh, I was just considering how different my daily life is

here. Chloe's as well. It will be difficult in some ways to leave here when the time comes."

"For me, too; I've been rambling around in this big house alone, since Christina died. I'll miss you."

Now they were both smiling as they finished preparing dinner.

CHAPTER 22

Though Penelope's mind was more at rest since she and Blaine had talked in the dining room, there were still other matters weighing on her. She missed her children terribly. She had never been away from them since their births. Now they were separated, not only by distance, but by time. The reality of that was nearly unfathomable. Additionally, she was still troubled over what Levi might have told them. And finally, as to her return, she was still at a loss as to how that would happen, given the memories of all those involved.

It was on this matter, she and Blaine were conversing one evening when a memory suddenly came to Blaine concerning the timekeeper.

"I think I know how Timothy plans to send you back without everyone thinking you have returned from the dead."

Penelope leaned forward on the sofa in anticipation of good news.

"Before Timothy and I came back to take you and Chloe from the fire, he insisted I rest. I had been awake for nearly twenty hours. Under the circumstances, I was not sure I could sleep or even if I should. Time was of the essence. But Timothy told me he would help by keeping time from me, whatever that meant. He said by doing that, I would sleep, but not dream or experience any kind of disturbance. That way, my body would get the rest it needed. Now, here's the strange part. I felt like I had slept for hours and was completely refreshed, but when I woke up, not one minute had passed since the time I had gone to sleep."

"That's fascinating, Blaine, but I'm not sure how that applies to my situation."

"Let me try to explain this. It's a bit complicated, but I'll do my best. You see, the only one who needs to believe you died is Levi Burke. For the others, it's better if they don't believe you and Chloe died. Timothy knows this. I think what Timothy is planning to do is wait for Levi's death. When that happens, I think he's going to remove the section of time when Levi returned home and saw me and everything that followed like the charges of witchcraft, the burning, and taking the children away. Actually, he would be removing the servants and the children from real time when those things happened. Therefore, they would have no memories of Levi's return or anything that followed. Not the servants or the children."

"So," Penelope said, trying to summarize, "one and a half days would simply vanish from the memories of the servants and my children."

"I think so, yes," Blaine said, "But Timothy can't make that change until after Levi dies. That's why you and Chloe need to be here for those 67 days. It also means that no matter what Levi tells the children, they won't even remember. It will be as though their father never came home that day, and they were never taken away. The only ones who will remember how things really were will be the four of us. Levi will have known, too, but by the time you and Chloe get back, he will be dead. That will be the end of it."

As complicated as it all seemed, it made sense to Penelope. She felt a tremendous weight lifted from her shoulders. Could it really be that simple for her to step back into her life? Only she and Chloe would know how close they had come to death. Only they would know what Levi Burke was capable of. Only they would recall all the marvelous and wondrous events and possibilities which lay ahead for Burkeshire Manor.

Blaine thought to himself how only he would know how completely devastating it had been when she *did* die and how lost and hopeless his future would have been without her.

What a mystery time was. How carefully one must choose his steps, always considering consequences. What an opportunity we all have for strength and growth, or, if we are careless, for sorrow and suffering. Not only our own, but the sorrow and suffering of others if we fail to see the impact we all have on the lives of those around us. Knowing this, one would surely choose more carefully the steps they take each day.

Jack made himself a regular visitor in the manor, although it was plain to see that his interest in Chloe had become a more powerful draw than simply visiting Blaine. Even now, they were out walking on the cliffs, enjoying a beautiful sunset. Both Penelope and Blaine were a bit concerned, knowing that in about five more weeks, Jack and Chloe would need to say goodbye, perhaps forever. They never questioned that they, Blaine and Penelope, would continue to see one another even after her return. The paintings indicated as much, although Blaine had continued to keep them hidden from view. But, for Jack and Chloe it did not appear to be ordained. At least, there was no evidence to indicate otherwise.

Another item of business which Blaine and Penelope had discussed that evening was the subject of clothing for the two women. While they both insisted there was sufficient clothing from Christina's wardrobe to sustain them through the next several weeks, particularly since they had learned to use the washer and dryer, there was the matter of the clothing they had arrived in. Their dresses had both been scorched by the fire and smelled of smoke. They could not be used again to wear on their return home.

Blaine decided a trip to town was in order. They would seek out the local fabric store, find appropriate patterns, probably in the costume pattern section, and make new dresses. Better yet, they would hire a seamstress to come to the manor for appropriate fittings and do the work for them.

Penelope was delighted by the idea. After sharing the idea with Chloe when she and Jack returned from their walk, it was decided in two days, on Saturday, they would take a trip to town. That's when Jack would have the day off and he could join them.

Privately, Blaine and Jack made plans to take them to a movie matinee. There was a Disney marathon happening at the cinema that weekend. Something animated would probably be the safest bet. Both were a little concerned that they wouldn't be able to grasp the difference between real and Hollywood if real actors were involved. And, of course, it had to be a modest movie without language, violence or nudity. They settled on the Lion King. The whole idea of a movie theater would be an experience in itself.

By the time Saturday rolled around, however, Blaine decided it would be best if he explained what a movie was to Penelope and Chloe before they went. This would be their first trip into town. There would be many more people than they had seen in the harbor, but by now Blaine figured they could handle it.

Jack arrived about ten that morning and the four of them set off in search of the fabric store. This was not familiar territory for either of the men, so all of them were a bit uneasy as they walked into Fabrics Galore on Second Street. Penelope surprised everyone when she walked immediately to the sales counter and spoke to the young woman there.

"Good morning, Miss. The two of us, (she motioned to

Chloe and herself) are looking for appropriate fabric for dresses to be worn to a costume party. We shall be dressed as women from the late 1600s. We shall also require the services of a seamstress to sew these dresses. Can you help us?"

Blaine and Jack gave each other looks that said they were impressed with her handling of the situation.

The young woman replied, "Let's begin by choosing the proper pattern, shall we? When we have found what you want, I'll send you back to Judy. She's our seamstress and she can give you her schedule."

Penelope cast a triumphant look Blaine's way; then she followed the young woman to the pattern drawers. Blaine and Jack followed at a distance, giving the ladies room to work, but staying close enough to assist if anything unexpected came up.

"Will you require costumes, too?" The young woman asked the men.

"No," Blaine said, "we already have ours."

While the women looked through patterns, Blaine took a few minutes to talk with Jack about Chloe. "Not to butt in," he said, "but you and Chloe seem to have hit it off pretty well."

"Yeah," Jack said. "She's... I don't know... kind of sweet. She's just so excited about the simplest things; easy to please. You know what I mean?"

Blaine knew exactly what he meant. "I just don't want to see you, well, you know. She's going to leave in a few weeks. Are you going to be okay with that?"

Jack was thoughtful for a minute, then said, "You know

as well as I that nothing in time is carved in stone. These few weeks may be all that we have, but this is the first time I've felt anything since my wife died. Let me ask you something. If you had known Christina would die three years after your wedding, would you have still married her?"

Blaine had asked himself that very question shortly after she died. His answer now to Jack was the same as it had been then.

"Absolutely. She was worth it."

"Chloe isn't going to die," Jack said. "She's just going away. But you, Blaine, you will be traveling to where she is from time to time. Who knows how things could turn out. Let's just see how it goes."

Blaine understood. He would not question Jack about it again.

The women had decided on a "costume" dress pattern. The young woman was now leading them back to Judy who would take over from here. Blaine assisted in the arrangements for her fee and helped schedule the times for fittings at the manor. He thought that would be better than running to town several more times. When all that was settled, Judy, Penelope and Chloe took another twenty-five minutes or so to select fabric, buttons, and lace. Petticoats would also be required. Finally, they browsed through a vintage clothing catalog to help them select appropriate footwear to complete the look.

In all, the time spent in the fabric shop took nearly an hour.

Both men heaved a sigh of relief as they stepped out onto the street.

"We have just under two hours until the movie starts," Jack said. "How about an early lunch?"

They decided on a deli with sidewalk seating because they would be indoors a good part of the afternoon. The women were also anxious to watch the passersby as they ate. It was just more than a week into June. The sky was crystal blue. The subtle scent of the ocean drifted in the air. Seagulls floated overhead, occasionally coming to rest nearby, hoping for a generous offering from those who were dining outside.

"I wish there was a way to capture all of this and save it forever," Chloe said.

"There is," Jack told her. He took out his cell phone and took several pictures of the street, the front of the deli, and each of them at the table, before he explained what he was doing. "This device does many things, including recording pictures. We can take them back and load them on Blaine's computer then print them out."

The women were lost after "recording pictures".

"I'll show you when we get home," Blaine said. He hadn't wanted to get into all of that computer stuff with them, but Jack left him no choice.

After lunch, they walked the few blocks to the theater because it was such a beautiful day. They were a bit early so they did not have to wait in line; however, they knew they would soon be overrun with children and their parents once movie time drew closer. They chose seating in the back so as not to disrupt the other viewers if the women had questions.

As they waited, Blaine explained the concept of moving pictures once again. He also let them know that they need only say so if they found the movie not to their liking.

When the movie began, they were both startled by the volume, but aside from that, they were riveted to the screen.

"Will the wonders of your time never cease?" Penelope whispered to Blaine.

There were no questions or comments beyond that point. They became quickly taken in by the story. Blaine heard her soft laughter at the hijinks of the characters, and even saw a silent tear as those tender moments as the story unfolded. He reminded her of Christina by the way she found beauty in all things, and yet, she was uniquely herself in many other ways. He began to realize how deeply she touched him.

Jack sat with his arm around Chloe like two high school kids on a date. They whispered softly to each other, clearly infatuated with one another.

As the movie came to a poignant end, Blaine found, without realizing it, that he had covered Penelope's hand with his. He removed it quickly as the lights came up, feeling like a guilty schoolboy. Still, the thought came to him that she had not removed her hand from his. It was bold behavior for a woman of her time. And, she was a married woman, at that.

They sat a while, letting the bulk of the children and parents leave the theater before attempting an exit of their own.

202 | LEDA OSBORNE

"That was simply wonderful," Penelope said. "What a charming and touching story. I so wish the children could have seen it. They would have been delighted."

It was just after three when they left the theater. Blaine and Jack offered to extend the day in town if either of them wanted to see more, but Penelope shook her head.

"I believe we have had enough excitement for one day," Penelope said, smiling. "I should like to finish the evening at home."

She didn't want to say anything to the others. It had, indeed, been a wonderful day, but seeing all the children at the theater made her long for her own children. She kept those longings to herself, however, not wanting to dampen the otherwise happy mood.

CHAPTER 23

Judy, the seamstress from Fabrics Galore, was scheduled to come up to the manor for fittings on Wednesday, and once or twice a week thereafter until the dresses were completed. Penelope chose a dress befitting her station as mistress of the manor, while Chloe's dress needed to be suitable for the role of personal maid to Penelope. Chloe didn't seem to mind the distinction. It was second nature to her. However, Penelope saw to it that Chloe's dress was quite becoming.

It was actually more distasteful to Jack to know that Chloe would be dressed as a maid. He had certainly never seen her in that way. He knew his feelings on the matter were foolish. Her clothing could not change who she had become in his eyes, but it troubled him nonetheless.

On the evening of the 56th day, he and Chloe walked along the cliffs as the sun began its fiery descent in the sky. They were both painfully aware that time was short. Jack had never imagined that two people could pack so much love into 56 days, yet here it was. He loved Chloe as deeply as he had loved Nancy, and he had told her so. She, in turn, had expressed the same depth of feelings for him.

"I shall never forget these days as long as I live," she whispered as they stood locked in an embrace. "And I shall never regret a moment of them."

"I'm not giving up," Jack said, his voice choked with emotion. "Anything is possible. We have to believe that."

Holding on to that hope, they pushed the prospect of a final goodbye out of their minds, spending every moment they could together. They talked little; embraced much; and laughed at every opportunity. If it must be the end, they wanted only pleasant memories to cling to.

Levi Burke, on the other hand, was realizing how few pleasant memories he had shared with his wife and his children. Perhaps he *had* been away too much. He had known his wife was lonely. He also knew in his heart that he had done nothing to rectify the situation. Indeed, he had put it out of his mind in favor of pacifying his own conscience by telling himself he was only thinking of her wellbeing and that of the children.

And, the children, well, that was also weighing on him. Since he had taken them to Boston, he had only seen them a few times in the past month and a half. Alex had been cold with little to say except to question when they could return to their mother. The girls were open to the idea of gifts; however, they squirmed out of reach if he attempted to embrace them. He realized he was a stranger to them; had been a stranger to them their whole lives. He began to realize he had forfeited everything for the sake of wealth and power.

Each night when he closed his eyes, he couldn't escape the sight of Penelope lashed to a tree, suffering a most horrific death by fire. He also could not escape the reality that it had been by his hand that his wife, the mother of his children, had died in such a way.

Day by day, these truths haunted him. Night after night, the visions tormented him. He began to lose his mental edge in business. He missed key meetings due to fatigue. He forgot important details of new ventures and fell into fits of anger towards those who reminded him. Levi Burke was unraveling, one thread at a time. The more he unraveled, the angrier he became. The angrier he became, the more things fell apart. People began whispering that he was becoming delusional and paranoid. Others thought he was no longer in control of his faculties. He had even begun to believe this was Chloe's fault.

Yes. She must have cursed him with these terrifying night visions. She must have cast some evil spell upon him to drive him to madness. This simple servant, who, in league with the devil, believed herself to be more powerful than the great Levi Burke. The more he considered the possibility, the more he believed it to be true.

The thought outraged him. He would not be manipulated

by a servant, or by the devil himself. He was above that. He was stronger and more cunning, even than the devil. He knew this to be true and none could convince him otherwise.

Believing now that he had solved the mystery of his "bad spell", as he referred to it, he was more determined than ever to demonstrate that he was more powerful than a witch. He could and would control the events in his own life. Feeling confident now that things would soon change for the better, he instructed his carriage driver to deliver him to the finest establishment in Boston. There, he would celebrate his defeat of the witch's curse by the power of his own might and cleverness, by indulging himself in a fine meal.

Though he sat alone at his table, onlookers watched discretely as they saw him talking to himself. They heard him congratulate himself in outsmarting the witch, and declare himself to be the most cunning of men.

He consumed a large meal of meat and bread and much wine. And when he had consumed enough food for two men, he made his way to his waiting carriage. In the hot sun of the one o'clock hour, he climbed with some difficulty into the carriage. As the driver set the horses in motion, Levi Burke slumped forward, grabbing first his arm, then his chest. Without a cry or a sound, Levi Burke died. His driver, still unaware, continued on their way.

The weeks had drifted by faster than Blaine would have liked, certainly faster than Chloe and Jack wanted. They tried to squeeze as much time as possible out of each day, wanting to make enough memories to last a lifetime, but hoping for a miracle that would give them a lifetime together. Only Penelope, found that time moved too slowly. She missed her children desperately, and while they would likely not remember this time of separation, they must still be living it now. Her heart ached for them and for herself.

There was another matter on Penelope's mind as well. She had given it considerable thought. It was not right in her mind, that such remarkable and extraordinary events as had occurred in the last year, should go unknown to the world outside their small circle. Something Jack had told her kept coming back to her. Something he had said about the journal. The more she considered it, the more certain she was that her idea was the right thing to do. Finally, one evening, only a week before it was time to return to her own time, she took Jack aside. She handed him an envelope, explaining the instructions that she had written inside.

"When the time comes," she said, "I'm counting on you to carry this out. Will you do that for me? It is my legacy."

Jack understood and agreed to do his part.

Blaine too, had done some serious pondering these last weeks. Consequently he had come to some decisions of his own. One of those decisions concerned a marker for Christina's grave. He now knew what he wanted. He contacted Ben Jacobson at the funeral home and discussed these final arrangements for her headstone. His final request of Ben was that it not be delivered

208 | LEDA OSBORNE

until at least August. By then, Blaine knew Chloe and Penelope would be back in their own time.

He had also considered Christina's final words to him before she died. "She can help you." Blaine knew without question that Christina had somehow known about Penelope and she wanted him to let her help him. Help him through his grief, help him keep his heart alive and not shut out the world. Help them to find friendship and perhaps even love again.

Penelope *had* helped him, and he believed he had helped her as well. Where there might have been two souls separated by time, lost in loneliness and isolation, there were now two souls touched by hope, wonder, companionship, and perhaps love. Their lives had been changed in ways they could never have imagined. Once, fanciful dreams were now real possibilities. The inconceivable had become the expected. Blaine believed he was now ready for whatever lay ahead.

Jack and Chloe were less hopeful for their futures, but both grateful for the time they had shared. As a servant, Chloe had never considered finding a love of her own. She was, she had thought, content to live vicariously through Penelope. But now, she had found what she thought was unattainable for herself. And though she knew it would soon come to an end, she was nonetheless grateful for the time they'd had. She would remember these days as long as she lived and they would sustain her.

Jack still clung to the hope that Timothy would find a way to keep them together, if not now, then perhaps someday in the future. He had to hang on to that hope. Without it, he would have to concede that soon it would simply be the end. How could it be the end when they had all seen that time changes everything? No. He would continue to hold onto that hope. It was the only way he could let her go.

So, the final week of this adventure, on day 60 of 67, each of them struggled with what to say to one another and what to do with their remaining time.

Blaine commented that he would get back to the work of restoring the manor. Jack said something about how he'd gotten behind on some paperwork at the department. Chloe made certain all of Christina's clothing was properly cleaned and returned to her closet, except for a few items to carry them through the next few days.

Their dresses for returning through time had been completed and hung ready in their rooms. The four of them sat, mostly without speaking, in the parlor this night.

Blaine finally shared a thought for all of them, but to no one in particular. "Have you ever wondered how often something like this happens? For all we know, this could be happening all over the world time and again, to other people just like us. Timothy did say that there were other timekeepers like him who had the ability to alter time within their own boundaries. And, he said he had done something like this countless times over the centuries and this was the first time he'd ever made a mistake. You know," he said to Penelope, "the part about you and Chloe dying. That was a mistake."

"I guess we would never really know," Jack said. "Each

time the timeline is changed, everyone would have a new set of memories to go along with it."

Penelope jumped in. "But Chloe and I will remember this time, will we not?"

"Yes," Blaine said. "Timothy told me the two of you would remember all of this."

Both women sighed with relief.

"There must be a reason," Jack said, "that each of us is allowed to remember these events. If there were not a reason to remember, then why not wipe all our memories clean the moment the two of you return to your own time?"

Chloe added her own thoughts as Jack had encouraged her to do. "Perhaps the reason we shall all remember is to provide contrast. Because of these memories, we will know how fortunate we are to have experienced these events compared to what might have been had we not had this experience. I, for one, shall never have known love." She slipped her hand into Jack's. "Knowing that makes me ever so much more grateful."

Blaine did not have to imagine the contrast. He knew how isolated and driven he had become before Christina's words finally convinced him to turn to Penelope. And he certainly would never forget the unimaginable horror of witnessing the deaths of Chloe and Penelope and how Penelope's spirit had haunted him.

Penelope also clearly saw the striking contrast between her life prior to meeting Blaine for the first time, and now. "Yes, Chloe's thought was a good one. Perhaps we all needed some contrast with which to provide proper perspective and develop gratitude for that which we all have gained."

The remaining days of the final week were spent in quiet contemplation and bittersweet moments of tenderness for Jack and Chloe.

Penelope's feelings were all over the map. Anxious to return home to her children and the world she knew and reluctance to leave the daily opportunity to be with Blaine. They had clearly drawn closer during hers and Chloe's period of hiding in his time. In spite of allowing him to hold her hand during the Lion King, she had not entirely forgotten that, at least for the present time, she was still a married woman. Nevertheless, she no longer questioned whether they would, when the time was right, become one another's salvation. Blaine and she would one day become lovers. Though their love would consist of only stolen moments through time, it would be held as one of the greatest loves of all time.

Well, let's not get ahead of ourselves. Blaine, that clever boy, had indeed figured out how I would get Penelope and Chloe back home. It was my intent to simply remove one event. Levi Burke would not return home to discover Blaine and would therefore not murder his wife and her maid. He was also correct that I could not remove this event except after Levi Burke had already died. That fateful day was now upon us. It was July 27, 1693. At 1:36 p.m., Levi Burke would step into a carriage in the hot sun, clutch his chest in pain and fall into death after having consumed a substantial lunch. Immediately following this event, I was free to remove that fateful day from history. I decided to give Blaine a little warning. Drawing from a popular sport of Blaine's day I felt it rather clever of myself when I whispered in Blaine thoughts the two hour warning. I suppose I shouldn't toot my own horn, concerning my own cleverness, however, when you consider the nature of my existence, if I don't, who will? I do so love the various nuances of humor in any given time.

Meanwhile, while those in 2017 said their goodbyes, I removed sections of May 19th, 20th and 21st from 1693. Mr. Wilmington no longer prepared to meet Mr. Burke at the docks with his wagon, for Mr. Burke would not arrive home that day. Therefore, all time changing events would no longer occur. As far as the servants knew, on July 27, 1693, Mrs. Burke and Chloe had been taking a walk along the cliffs and would return soon. The children would be in the library attending to their lessons. Only Chloe and Penelope would ever know any different.

I must admit, I was rather pleased with myself at this point in time. In spite of the difficulties along the way, everything was going to work out just as it should.

CHAPTER 24

It was about 11:30 on the morning of the 67th day. Blaine was preparing a light lunch with Penelope's help. Jack had taken the day off to be with Chloe as long as possible. They were sitting together in the parlor while Penelope and Blaine worked in the kitchen. Suddenly Blaine stopped working.

"Did you hear that?" he asked Penelope.

"I heard nothing," she said.

"It was Timothy. He just told me we had two hours. I think he meant two hours before you and Chloe leave."

Penelope also stopped working. She was both excited to see her children and sad that her time here was nearly gone. "We should tell Jack and Chloe," she finally said.

They went to the parlor together to share the news. For Jack and Chloe there were no mixed feelings. It was sad news.

"We must go upstairs and dress," Penelope encouraged her gently.

Chloe nodded in agreement and followed Penelope out of the room.

When they had gone, Blaine said, "I'm sorry Jack. I know this is hard for both of you."

Jack stretched his legs and lean back with his arms reaching overhead. "What can we do? Apparently Timothy is in control of the situation. I had hoped he would let her stay, but I guess Penelope will need her there. There must be a reason."

Blaine knew nothing he could say would help, so he said nothing.

When the women returned a few minutes later, dressed in the proper attire for their time, the four of them sat down to the lunch which had been prepared. No one seemed very hungry, nibbling at their food with little interest.

Penelope thought how her husband must, at this very moment, be facing his own death. In spite of his hand in her death, she found she could not hold bitter feelings for him. He had treated her more than fairly given the circumstances of their marriage, at least until that last day. She could expect no more.

Jack and Chloe cast one another silent messages of love as they ate. Both tried to hold onto the feeling of gratitude for the time they had been given, but it was difficult now that her departure was imminent.

Looking at the two of them in the clothing of their own time, Blaine felt the harsh reminder that they were, indeed, from two different worlds, past and present. In truth, they should never have met. They most certainly would never have had any impact on each other's lives. Yet, in defiance of all logic, these things had occurred. His eyes, his mind and his heart could not deny it.

Blaine looked at the clock. Nearly an hour of their two remaining hours had already passed.

"It shall be wrong if we were to suddenly appear within the walls of the manor," Penelope said, "I believe we should walk out on the cliffs to ensure we are not in view when we return."

Everyone nodded in agreement.

"I must collect my pictures," Chloe said. "I want to take them with me."

Penelope also wanted the photos that had been taken when Melissa was there.

While the two women left to collect their keepsakes, Jack and Blaine cleaned up the nearly untouched lunch. Jack kept looking at the clock. It was now 12:45.

On impulse, Blaine pulled two beers out of the fridge and handed one to Jack.

"For the road," he said.

Jack accepted the beer, twisted off the top and chugged nearly half of the bottle before stopping to breathe.

"Damn! I don't want her to go."

"I can bring messages from you each time I go back," Blaine offered, "but I know it won't be the same. At least the two of you can keep up."

Jack said nothing, but walked into the great room to wait for the women.

When the two women joined them in the great room, Chloe motioned that their treasured photographs were tucked securely in the pocket of her apron. Penelope, of course, not being a servant, was not wearing an apron and had no pockets.

The four of them slowly made their way outside, walking up to the cliffs and then westward toward the trees.

It was a beautiful July day, nearly August. The air was warm. The breeze off the water was light. For some reason it reminded Penelope of the night she and Chloe were being walked to their death. She held the same feelings of calm and dread at the same time. It was a sense of the end, somehow. It was certainly the end of her stay in Blaine's time and perhaps she was also sensing the end of her loveless marriage. Then there was an end for Chloe and Jack that hung in the air. She hope that those were all the endings she was feeling.

When they reach the trees, they stopped walking. It would be safe for Penelope and Chloe to suddenly appear here in their own time.

According to the time of Timothy's two hour warning, they had about twenty minutes left.

"When you get back," Blaine was saying to Penelope, "and after word of Levi's death reaches the household, will you try to explain me to them?"

"I don't know. Perhaps they would think me mad."

"Maybe. But if Chloe could back you up, it would sure make it easier if someone saw me when I came."

"I shall have to give that some thought. Meanwhile, we should be careful."

"I just don't want a repeat of what happened before. I worry for you."

"Perhaps Timothy could be of some help in that regard. Perhaps you could ask him," Penelope said.

Jack and Chloe stood a short distance away embracing one another in silence.

"Whatever happens," Penelope said, "I shall always be grateful to you, Blaine. You have brought me a new life in every way possible. I shall cherish every moment we have shared."

"Me too," Blaine said in his clumsy way. "I've needed this, and Christina knew I would. I don't know how she knew, but she knew we needed each other." He went beyond the propriety of her day and pulled her into an embrace. "I'll miss having you here."

Penelope did not resist. They embraced as the minutes ticked by. Then, without sound or shudder, the two women simply vanished.

Jack and Blaine looked at one another. There were no words. Both men stood silently turning to look out to sea. After a few minutes, Jack took a step toward Blaine then stopped suddenly. He stooped down to retrieve something on the ground.

"What is it?" Blaine asked.

"It's the photos. The ones Chloe had in her pocket. I wonder if they fell out."

"I don't think so," Blaine said. "I don't think Timothy allowed them to go back. They weren't meant to exist in that time."

Jack tucked them into a shirt pocket without comment as he and Blaine walked silently back to the house.

Chloe and Penelope appeared near the trees where they had been standing. Chloe broke into sobs as Penelope tried to comfort her.

"My dear Chloe. I am so sorry for the loss you are feeling. You must try to pull yourself together. We must return to the house now, in hopes of finding all is well. Are you ready?" she asked, wiping away the tears from her cheeks.

"Yes, Ma'am, I'm ready."

The two of them walked at a casual pace toward the manor. As they reach the kitchen door, they paused, looked at each other, took deep breaths and walked in.

Mrs. Wilmington and Millie were in the kitchen.

"I was getting concerned," Mrs. Wilmington said. "You were out walking a very long time. Chloe, the children are in the library awaiting their afternoon lessons. You should attend to them promptly," she scolded.

Penelope's eyes lit up. She grabbed Chloe by the hand and nearly ran to the library. She flung open the doors and hurried inside.

"Oh, my darlings!" she exclaimed. "I'm so happy to see you!"

"We're waiting for our story," little Ingrid said. "Where were you, Chloe?"

"She was walking with me," Penelope answered quickly. "I'm sorry I kept her so late."

Chloe was still trying to get her bearings. "Which book were we reading, again?" she asked, as innocently as possible.

"This one," Alex said, handing her a thick volume.

"Oh, yes. Well, then, shall we begin?"

Penelope sat and listened with the children. She simply wanted to be near to them after such a long separation, although they were clearly unaware of such a separation. *"Thank you Timothy"* she thought to herself. *"I shall be forever grateful."*

Penelope's eyes drifted slowly around the familiar library. A part of her was truly happy to be home again. Another part of her considered how very far in time they had traveled to get home. Blaine, Jack, the harbor and the town of Machias were many generations away. It was almost as though she had dreamed the whole thing. Time travel. What a completely irrational idea. But all she had to do was look at Chloe's face with the faint tracks of tears on her cheeks, and at the dresses they wore, made by a woman who wouldn't be born for nearly 300 years. It had been real; every bit of it!

In a few days, a message would reach the manor that Levi Burke had died. What would the children feel? She was sad to realize that the girls would only miss the gifts he brought. Alex may feel more betrayed than sad. Dying would be seen as the final insult to Alex. Another way to avoid being here and being the father he should have been. Penelope would do her best to be sensitive to those feelings.

And how would she react? She didn't believe the servants were naïve enough to expect her to be brokenhearted and inconsolable; however, she would respectfully mourn the news. After all, they did not know that he had recently been capable of murder.

Jack and Blaine were experiencing a bit of déjà vu, only with the roles reversed. Jack was doing the pouring, most of the drinking, and talking while Blaine listened at the kitchen table. Though Chloe had not died, she may as well have. There was nothing in the journal or paintings to indicate that he would ever see her again. He was now chiding himself loudly for ever having allowed himself to care for her so deeply. Not only was it hurtful for him, but it was terribly unfair to Chloe.

Blaine only listened, not saying much. That was fine with Jack. For the moment he seemed content to be angry at himself and didn't want to be talked out of it.

To tell the truth, Blaine was hardly listening. He was thinking about how things might have gone when they returned. He hoped his theory of how Timothy would adjust time to work them back in was correct. If so, things would have gone well and her children would be there. He had to believe that was the case. Surely Timothy wouldn't send them back to anything less.

"Hey, Blaine. Are you listening?" Jack was saying

"Oh, sorry, man. I was just hoping everything went okay when the girls got back."

"Yeah, me too. I think I'm going to head home. I'm not doing anyone any good sitting here drinking myself stupid."

"You want a lift?"

"No. I'm not that far gone. I'll see you in a few days, okay?"

Blaine walked with him to the door.

"Okay, Jack. Take care of yourself. I'm here if you need anything."

"Sure. Bye."

CHAPTER 25

It's true that not all came through this change with perfect happiness; however, saving Penelope and Chloe was the primary goal. In that sense, it was mission accomplished. Unfortunately, both Jack and Chloe were feeling rather low. As I have said previously, I provide time. What mortals do with that time is not under my control. In this case, each of them knew their time would be limited. Nevertheless, I do feel a bit sad for them. Perhaps things would unfold in such a way that I could provide some assistance. I would keep it in mind.

As for Penelope, she was nothing short of elated to have been reunited with her children. She made the most of their reunion, even though the children didn't know it was a reunion. Indeed, they were somewhat overwhelmed at the sudden abundance of time and affection their mother showered on them. It was truly beautiful to behold.

Then, of course, came the day, shortly after she and Chloe had returned, when the news of Levi's death reached the manor. Though Penelope did her best to show a degree of respectful mourning, she was not surprised to find that she was the only one. The girls hardly gave it a thought. Little Ingrid's only comment was, "Does this mean he won't bring us more presents?" Alex responded in a manner very much as Penelope had expected. He was clearly disturbed, but said only, "He was never here anyway."

The staff had taken care of every need at the manor for years without his help. There was plenty of money and supplies would continue to arrive in the manner they always had. Except for some polite words of respect, nothing really changed. Levi's body had been prepared and delivered back to the manor. Mr. Wilmington and the men had dug a grave and an appropriate head stone had been ordered, however it was not expected to arrive for several months. Aside from those details, there was little change in the routine of the manor.

There was, however, a change in Penelope Burke. After Levi's death, she seemed to come to life. It began in little ways at first. Penelope wandered into the kitchen one day to inquire about what was being prepared for dinner that evening. To Miss Millie's astonishment, Penelope asked if she could help prepare the meal.

"Are my preparations unacceptable?" Millie asked, clearly concerned.

"Of course not, Millie. You are a wonderful cook. I simply

thought I would enjoy working in the kitchen from time to time. I found it very satisfying when I was younger. I often cooked alongside my mother. May I cook with you tonight?"

Millie's smile was so broad it nearly covered half of her face. "Yes, Ma'am, I would enjoy that as well."

There were other changes. Penelope asked Mr. Wilmington to have the men help him in moving the piano from the library to the great room. She declared to the staff that at least one evening each week there would be music and dancing in the great room. Everyone was invited and asked to participate. She also decided the children should be taught the finer points of dance. This new arrangement was met with many smiles and much participation. Of course, only she and Chloe knew where this idea came from.

The most startling change was Penelope's decision concerning meals. There were only the children and herself in that large dining room. She decided that once a meal was ready, the Burkes and the staff should eat together. They had all lived at the manor for as long as they had been there, and she felt there was no reason they should not share meals together. They would still eat in the dining room because of their numbers, but Penelope felt it would be an excellent time to build better relationships with each of them. It was also an excellent time to discuss the needs of the manor. Of course, she was still afforded the respect due as the mistress of the manor, and she would accept nothing less, but in many ways, they *were* a family. After a few weeks of this arrangement,

Penelope noticed how it lifted the spirits of all those who called the manor home.

All of these changes occurred within two months of her return home. Always in the back of her mind was Blaine. She wondered when he would come again. She wondered, also, if he would suddenly appear within the house, causing another disturbance. However, she didn't really believe Timothy would make that mistake again.

She was correct. I would not. In fact, I had given some thought as to how I would proceed with Blaine's visits and had made some decisions.

Meanwhile, Blaine had been doing some wondering as well. Penelope had been gone for two months. Within his own time, if someone was gone for two months, you could pick up a phone and call them; send them an email or snail mail; or even send them a text. But for him and Penelope, there was only one method of communication, time travel.

It was late September again. More than a year had passed since he and Christina had come to Burkeshire Manor. Somehow it seemed longer. So much had happened.

Jack stopped in about once a week to see if Blaine had traveled yet, but he was trying to keep busy with extra hours at work. Jack knew he was doing what he had done when Nancy died, but he didn't care. He did it anyway. He missed Chloe so much. It just didn't seem fair that he should lose her like this.

To Jack's credit, he did not resent Blaine for his ability to travel back and see Penelope, though it had not yet happened since they had returned. He was truly happy for him. He knew Blaine couldn't do anything to change what had happened, or what would happen. He valued Blaine's friendship too much to make this an issue between them. It was just so damned hard.

It was about this time when I decided to pay Blaine a visit. I figured he had already seen me; been out of time with me; and helped me change a time line. What harm could it do to make him an occasional exception to the rule of anonymity?

When I came to him he was lying against the pillows of his bed, drinking a beer and examining Penelope's paintings which had been re-hung in the master suite.

"Hello, Blaine. May I join you?"

Blaine was so startled, he spilled beer all over himself and the blankets. He looked toward the sound of Timothy's voice and found him standing near the bedroom door.

"A little warning would be nice," he said, though he wasn't really annoyed. He was actually glad to see him. "How did everything go for Penelope and Chloe? I've been worried for two months."

"Splendidly! No one but Penelope and Chloe knows what really happened. She's been blossoming like a rose and it's all because of her stay here with you. You should see the changes she's made."

Blaine was relieved. He had assumed everything was fine,

but it was good to know for sure. "What kind of changes?" he asked.

"I think I'll let her tell you."

"So, are you here to take me back?"

"Not yet, but that's what I want to discuss. Do you remember when you asked me if you could choose when you go back?"

"Yeah. Does this mean I can?"

"No, but I am willing to work with you. First I need you to understand that I am still the one in charge of travel, but there are things we can do to make it both easier for you and safer for Penelope."

"Easier and safer sounds good to me. What's the plan?"

"Good. The first thing you'll need to do is call that seamstress and get some clothing made for yourself. You'll need appropriate clothing. Second, there will be no more surprise entries and exits. The same way I whispered the two hour warning to you when I sent the ladies back, I will warn you with enough time to dress appropriately and be ready to go. Let's say about thirty minutes."

"Wow. Sounds like you've been thinking about this. Anything else?"

"Yes. Each time I send you back I will send you to the road below the manor. To avoid witnesses, I will vanish you from there also by giving you another warning that you are about to leave. I'll give you about fifteen minutes to get to that location."

"What if I can't get there in time?"

"Then you run the risk of disappearing in front of those who shouldn't see. My point is, be there on time. We don't need another fly in the ointment. By coming and going on the road, you may pose as a gentleman from the small group of settlers which are beginning to set up residence near the harbor. Or perhaps you may claim to be a merchant who comes by periodically. I shall let you and Penelope decide. Under the cover of such a story, you may visit with or court Penelope in front of others in the house. That is the extent of the help I can give you. The two of you will have to make it work. Agreed?"

"Sounds great, Timothy. When can I go?"

"As soon as you are properly attired. Not before that."

Blaine was disappointed, but he knew this was for Penelope's safety. "Then I had better get hold of that seamstress right away."

Even as he spoke those words, Timothy had vanished.

"Not much on long goodbyes, I guess. Thanks, Timothy," he said to nothing but empty space.

Blaine picked up the phone to dial Jack's number. It went to voice mail. "Hi, Jack," he said after the beep, "I'm just calling to let you know Timothy was just here. The girls are fine. Call me."

Jack must have been screening calls. When he heard the message from Blaine, he called back right away. "Hey, Blaine, it's about time. I was beginning to wonder if we dreamed the whole thing. What did he say?"

"I hear you. I was getting a little worried, too. He said

everything went great and the girls are doing well. Mostly he came by to say he had some new guidelines for me about… traveling. I don't think we should discuss the details on the phone. C'mon by after you're off tomorrow. We can talk then."

"That'll be early. I've got the late shift tonight. How about I meet you for lunch?"

"Okay. One o'clock at Maxine's. I have a costume to pick out at the fabric store first."

"That sounds like a story to me. I'll see you at one."

Chloe and Penelope tucked the children in together that evening as Penelope had done since their return. When all was secure, Chloe joined Penelope in her room, one floor down.

"It's been two months, Chloe. What could the timekeeper be waiting for?"

"Perhaps he was allowing for proper time to mourn Mr. Burke," then added under her breath, "Bloody waste of time that would be, if you ask me."

Penelope considered scolding Chloe for that comment, but found herself letting go a soft chuckle instead. "I believe all mourning has come to an end."

On the day they had returned, Chloe had been distressed to discover that the photos had not made it back with them. The women came to the same conclusion Blaine had. They simply weren't meant to exist in this time.

In an effort to comfort Chloe somewhat, Penelope was making an attempt of a painting of Chloe and Jack together.

Chloe was, of course, able to serve as a model for herself, and was very helpful in remembering the specific contours and details of Jack's face since she had clearly observed him with far greater focus than Penelope had. Chloe sat now, as Penelope added more detail to the painting.

"Do you think we shall see each other again?" Chloe asked wistfully.

"We have no way of knowing; however, I believe false hope is more cruel than truth. I do not believe you will meet again. That is my feeling."

"Sadly," Chloe replied, "I share that feeling. We both knew it couldn't last, but we believed it was worth it for the time we had."

"And do you still believe it was worth it?"

"I do."

"Then it was, and I shall never allow you to believe otherwise."

"And if the timekeeper never allows Blaine to return here, will it have been worth it for you?"

Penelope's heart felt a tug at the thought of Blaine never returning. Still, would it have been worth it? The answer came to her lips with no hesitation. "It most certainly would have been worth it. Every minute."

Both women fell silent as poser and painter considered the very real possibility that both their adventures may have indeed come to an end.

CHAPTER 26

The following day, Blaine met Jack at Maxine's after stopping first at the fabric store and arranging for Judy to prepare a few items of appropriate clothing for his travels through time.

Jack looked hopeful as Blaine slid into the booth where he sat waiting. "So, tell me, what did Timothy have to say?"

"He said they were both doing fine. No one at the manor seemed to remember anything. The children were there as though they had never left, and they just stepped back into their lives as though they had never been gone. He did say that Penelope had made some changes at the manor after her return, but he wanted to wait and let her tell me what they were."

"What about Chloe? Is she okay?"

"I don't know anything except that they're fine. It seemed the main purpose of his visit was to tell me how he had worked out my visits for the future. He wanted me to have that seamstress, Judy, make me some appropriate clothing to wear. He also said he would give me a warning each time I traveled so that I could dress properly before I went. He would then give me another warning before it was time to come back so I could get to a pre-arranged location before I disappeared. It seemed like he had given this a lot of thought so we don't run into any more problems."

"That's good. I don't suppose he said anything about me and Chloe being able to get together again, did he?

Blaine felt compassion rising within himself for Jack. Jack was trying desperately to be an interested and supportive friend as Blaine described the timekeeper's visit, while inside he was hoping against hope to hear some good news regarding himself and Chloe. Surely, through all of this, the timekeeper had found a way to give them more time together.

"I'm sorry, Jack. He just finished what he had come to tell me and then vanished. I didn't even get a chance to ask about you two."

"Sure," Jack said. "I understand. Maybe he just hasn't had time to work that part out yet."

Jack's emphasis on the word *time* did not escape Blaine. He knew there was nothing he could say to make Jack feel better, so he simply shrugged and said nothing.

The waitress came and took their order, temporarily interrupting Jack's feelings of frustration, then they were alone again.

THE TIMEKEEPER'S TAPESTRY | 233

"What a ride," Jack said, seeming to be himself again. "Who would have thought such things could happen. If we weren't here to remind each other that all of this was real, well, I think a person could go crazy if they had to carry this secret all alone. Maybe that's why Chloe needs to be there with Penelope and we need to be here for each other."

"I'm really grateful to you, Jack. Not just because I can share this with you, but because you were there for me when Christina died."

"Well, what are friends for? There is something you can do for me, though." Jack reached into his jacket pocket and pulled out an envelope. "Next time you go back, will you bring this letter to Chloe? I don't even know if it will make it back with you. I know the pictures didn't, but a letter isn't a product of technology. Maybe it will work."

"Sure. We can give it a shot."

While they ate their lunch, they spent the time reminiscing about the times the four of them had shared. Jack even managed a few laughs as they remembered the innocence and awe with which the two women had met each new experience.

When they had finished their lunch, Blaine said, "I know you worked last night and haven't slept yet. Why don't you go get some rest, but stay in touch. I'll keep you up on anything new, and I'll get this to Chloe," he added, patting the letter in his pocket.

It was just over two weeks later when the first of Blaine's new wardrobe was ready. Judy was under instructions to complete the rest ASAP.

True to his word, Timothy did not make Blaine wait once he could be properly attired. The following morning Blaine received his thirty minute warning to get ready. He quickly dressed in his period clothing and, referencing men's hair styles he had seen on line for the late 1600's, he attempted to arrange his hair appropriately. When he was ready, he made his way down the driveway until he was out of view of the house.

For the previous two weeks, he had considered the cover story he would use. He had decided he would walk right up to the front door and present himself as a friend from Penelope's youth, prior to her marriage to Levi Burke. He would say he had come to extend his condolences after learning of the death of her husband. A few minutes after having situated himself along the road below the manor, Blaine found himself, at last, in the year 1693.

With Jack's letter tucked safely in his waistcoat, he made his way to the manor.

Mrs. Wilmington opened the door. She looked suspiciously at the young man before her. She did not try to conceal her suspicion. "Who are you and what is your business here?"

Blaine was about to put his acting skills to the test. "Good morning, Madam. My name is Blaine Michael Duncan. Mrs. Burke and I have been acquainted since childhood, though we have not seen one another in many years. When I heard the dreadful news of her husband's passing, I felt compelled to pay my respects. May I see her?"

Blaine was rather pleased by his performance, though Mrs. Wilmington still looked suspicious. Fortunately, Penelope had been standing at the top of the stairs when she heard someone at the door. She had witnessed Blaine's entire performance and found it difficult to contain her amusement and delight at seeing him dressed in clothing to match her time and especially the way he had combed his hair.

She threw herself into the charade with great enthusiasm.

"Blaine, my dear friend," she gushed as she hurried down the stairs. "It has been many years indeed. I am delighted you have come to visit me in this most trying time. Mrs. Wilmington, may I present my childhood friend, Mr. Duncan."

Mrs. Wilmington relinquished her guard dog position and stepped aside to allow Blaine to enter.

"I shall receive him in the parlor. Oh, and Mrs. Wilmington, would you fetch Chloe? I wish for her to join us for a few moments."

"Shall I bring some tea, Ma'am?"

"Yes, that would be delightful."

Blaine and Penelope stepped into the parlor and Penelope closed the doors behind them. When they were at last alone, both broke into laughter at their performances.

"Are you mad?" Penelope said, still smiling. "Coming to the front door as bold as can be. Look at you, your clothing and hair..."

"Do you like it?" he said, striking a pose. "It was Timothy's idea. There's more but I'll tell you about that in a few minutes. First, I just want to say, it is wonderful to see you again. I have missed you."

"I have missed you as well. I was afraid Timothy had decided it was too dangerous for us to see one another again. I am delighted to know that was not the case."

There was a light rap on the door and Chloe stepped in. When she saw Blaine, her eyes widened with delight. "How wonderful to see you," she said. "Did you come alone?" Though she had not been specific, both Penelope and Blaine knew she was hoping to see Jack as well.

By way of answer to her question, Blaine said, "He asked me to give this to you." He removed the letter from his waistcoat and passed it to Chloe's waiting hands.

Taking the letter, she then embraced Blaine briefly. "I am so grateful you were able to return. We have missed you." With that, she left the parlor, making her way upstairs where she could read her letter undisturbed.

Mrs. Wilmington brought their tea, then left them to visit.

Penelope began to bring Blaine current on the events of their return and the changes she had made at the manor since then. Blaine was especially happy to hear of the weekly music and dancing. She also explained that the photos had not made it back with them and how distressed Chloe had been. She asked if they were still with him and he assured her they were and had been kept safe. She told of the painting she was making for Chloe of her and Jack so that she would have something to remember him by.

When she had finished, Blaine explained Timothy's last visit and how these plans had been made concerning his clothing and cover story. Penelope loved the idea.

"I still only get about a fifteen minute warning before I have to go back, but if we're careful, we can work with that."

"We'll need to work out some details of your story," Penelope said, "but it will make things much less stressful this way. It's a wonderful plan. Perhaps Timothy could provide you with a horse and small carriage while you're here. It would be more believable than walking from below."

As they sat talking, Blaine took in the elegance of the room around him. He had not yet seen this room on previous visits.

"It seems strange, sitting in your parlor in your time. I guess it's my turn to be the guest again."

"Do you know how long you'll be able to stay now?"

"Timothy never really said, only that I would get a warning when it was near time to go. I believe, though, that if he has arranged for me to mingle with the house staff, he is probably expanding the length of time I get to stay."

"Yes. It would appear odd for you to come all this way to stay for only a few minutes. I agree, you will likely have longer visits."

They passed the time for nearly an hour to develop his cover story with appropriate details, and to simply visit with one another. Once again there was a soft rap on the door and Chloe came in. It was apparent she had been crying, no doubt over the letter Jack had sent, however she smiled sweetly as she passed her own letter to Blaine.

"I would be grateful if you would take this letter to Jack," she said. "I hope I shall see you again soon."

"I would be happy to, Chloe. Whatever I can do."

When Chloe left the room, Blaine said to Penelope, "It's Timothy. He says I need to go."

"So soon," Penelope said. "I shall walk you out."

Penelope walked with Blaine until they were away from view of the house. Blaine leaned forward without hesitation this time and kissed Penelope softly on the lips. She also did not hesitate to return his kiss.

"Come back soon," she whispered, and then he was gone.

CHAPTER 27

As I said at the very beginning of this story, it may be said that I am able to craft masterpieces of love, honor, justice, courage and destiny in the work that I do. As I have also said, I must take my work quite seriously, for missteps in time could beget catastrophic results.

As much as I would have loved to have given Chloe and Jack a lifetime together, it simply would not have been possible. The reasons why are simply too extensive in terms of life impacts to explain so I will not attempt to do so.

Now that my recent misstep had been corrected, Blaine and Penelope were able to enjoy many more years of visits in time. Their relationship took on a new life after the death of Levi Burke. Penelope no longer felt bound by her marriage vows and it wasn't long before they confessed their love for one another.

I was able and willing to lengthen their visits so that they had many hours together each time. I rather liked Penelope's idea of a horse and carriage and was able to *borrow* one and have it waiting there for Blaine's future visits. As far as the staff knew, he was a young gentleman from Mrs. Burke's past who came visiting Mrs. Burke from time to time. I could not grant him his request to choose the times he went, however, granting him a foreknowledge of both his leaving and arriving seemed to help significantly. It was the first time in all my centuries that I had worked this closely with a mortal. In this case, it seemed to work out quite successfully.

Blaine did finish the restoration of the entire house, however he never really opened it up as a bed-and-breakfast. Occasionally he would offer historic tours and on some occasions he would make it available for a family reunion, weddings or similar events.

He had special, sealed frames made for each of Penelope's paintings to preserve them from further deterioration. They still hung in the master suite which he kept for his own.

Under the guise of a family friend, he was accepted and liked by the staff of the manor. He was, after a time, able to spend time with the children as well.

In their hearts, Penelope and Blaine wished they could be married, but each knew there would be too many questions when he could not be found for long periods of time. It just wouldn't work.

Though Chloe was happy for the two of them, she often pined for Jack as he did for her, however many letters were sent forward and back through the years. Blaine did his best to keep them informed of one another, but as Jack had said to Blaine the day they left," it just wasn't the same."

As the years passed by, Blaine saw the passing of Mr. Wilmington at the age of 68 and his wife shortly thereafter. He saw Alex grow to manhood and leave the manor to take over where his father had left off. Penelope arranged for two trips each year for the girls to visit the city for social interaction, plays and musical performances. At this time they were also pleased to meet and visit with their grandparents who were quite elderly by then. One day, each of the girls as well as Alex would marry and have families of their own. But always, Penelope remained at Burkeshire Manor.

Some thirty years after Penelope and Chloe's return to the manor of their day, Blaine began to fall ill. Upon examination, he was found to have cancer. It was sad to see this, as he was yet a young man of 66, however I knew this would come. The cancer would grow quickly and become quite debilitating. I came to Blaine at this time for I wanted to let him know what a pleasure it had been partnering with him all these years. I also told him I would give him one more visit for an entire 12 hours so that he could explain the situation and say his goodbyes. It was all that I could offer.

For my part, the story ended there, however some mortals are outstanding beyond my expectations.

Blaine and Penelope had a love that quite literally tran-scended time, and in spite of my belief that all this was about to come to an end, they had figured out how to keep their story alive and moving throughout time.

I shall never forget either of them. They restored my faith in the potential of all mortals. Their love and courage were a shining example to those who came after them. Behold their cleverness for yourself. The remainder of this story was created by them.

SEPTEMBER 12, 2046

Melissa Sturgis flipped through her mail until she came across a letter that stood out from the others. It was a manila envelope from a Jack Rush of Machias Bay, Maine.

"I wonder what this is," she said aloud.

Her son looked up from the puzzle he was working with his children. "What is that, Mom?" He asked with mild interest.

"I'm not sure, Alex. It's from a man named Jack Rush in Maine. I haven't been to Maine since before you were born. Probably thirty years."

Alex got up from the table to take a closer look as she opened the envelope. She tipped the envelope to empty the contents onto the counter. There were two items. The first was a letter and the second was an airline ticket.

"What in the world?" she said. She unfolded the letter and began reading it aloud.

Dear Melissa Sturgis,

My name is Jack Rush. I'm executor of the estate for Mr. Blaine Michael Duncan of Machias Bay, Maine. You have been named in his will. Your presence is requested at Burkeshire Manor at 2 p.m. on Friday, September 20, 2046, for the reading of the will.

Melissa paused a moment. "Blaine Michael Duncan. Yes, I remember him. We met only once many years ago when I was researching our family history. But I don't understand. We only spent an hour or so together while he showed me the inside of the Manor." She continued reading.

Enclosed you will find a round-trip airline ticket for your convenience. It is my sincere desire you will attend. Please confirm your intention to attend by calling the number listed below.

Sincerely,

Jack Rush

Executor of the Duncan estate

207 555-6371

"Wow, Mom; you're going to go, aren't you?"

Melissa was still a bit stunned. She picked up the ticket and turned it over in her hands while she thought. "It doesn't say anything about your father attending," she said. "I wonder what he will say."

"What can he say?" Alex said. "You've been named in this guy's will. You have to go."

"Your father will be home soon. We'll talk about it then."

"Well, I'm calling the girls," Alex said. "This is pretty exciting stuff. I think they should know."

"I have a better idea. Why don't you invite Miriam and Darcy for dinner with us here tonight? Have them bring the whole family. We'll discuss this together."

That evening when the entire Sturgis family had gathered together, there were Melissa's three children, Alex, Miriam, and Darcy, named for their ancestors at Burkeshire Manor, their spouses, and eight grandchildren between them. David Sturgis, her husband, called the family to order so that Melissa could read the letter once again.

Her family nearly all spoke at once. "You have to go, Mom. How can you even hesitate? This man owns the home of our great-grandparents. That must be the reason you were contacted."

"I agree with the children," David said. "Go! I'll be fine here. You'll only be gone a few days. Just be sure to let us know what's happening."

It was decided. Melissa was happy and grateful for her family's support. Six days later she was on a plane, two days before the day of the reading.

Jack was happy she had chosen to come and even happier she had come early. There was so much to discuss. He had been preparing for this since a week before Penelope had returned to her own time thirty years ago, and yet he was still struggling with the things he would now be sharing. But this had been Penelope's instructions to him on that night long ago, and his intent was to do as she wished. In the thirty years since Penelope had made this request of him, Blaine had also discussed it with Penelope on his many visits with her. Eventually, they were in agreement. This was how they both wanted it. And so, Jack was now here to fulfill their wishes.

Jack sent a car to pick up Melissa at the airport on the 18th and instructed the driver to bring her directly to the manor, where he was waiting.

When the driver reached the manor, he pulled directly to the front doors and left the motor running as he opened Melissa's door for her. He then took her suitcase from the trunk and brought it to the front door as well.

"Oh, no," Melissa said. "I will be staying in town."

"These are my instructions, Ma'am. Mr. Rush is having you stay here."

Before she could protest further, he was back in the car and driving away. There was nothing left to do but ring the bell.

Almost immediately the door opened. A gray-haired gentleman in his mid-to-late 70's stood smiling at her.

"Melissa Sturgis," he said. "I would know you anywhere. Please come in."

"Have we met?" she asked.

"No, but you are the image of your grandmother. Please, let me bring you something to drink. Coffee? Tea? A cocktail perhaps?"

"Coffee would be fine. Thank you. Did you know my grandmother?" she asked.

"Let's take a seat in the parlor," he said, ignoring her question. "I'll be right back with our coffee. We have a lot to discuss."

When he returned to the parlor he set the tray between them on the coffee table and took a seat on the sofa facing her. He began, "This visit his been many years in the making. I hope you will bear with me. This is a story which must be told from the beginning. It is also a story which must be heard with an open mind and heart. It was not only Blaine Duncan's wish that I share this with you, but it was also the wish of your great, great grandmother, Penelope Whittier Burke. Are you ready to begin?"

Melissa felt she was being primed. She nodded hesitantly.

"I shall begin by reading a letter to you written by the hand of your great, great grandmother, Penelope Whittier Burke. Keep in mind that I will explain how this can be as we go along. For now, I simply ask that you trust me and keep an open mind."

Melissa sipped her coffee and waited as Jack unfolded a letter which he had carefully removed from inside the cover of a very old book. It appeared to be a journal. He began reading.

My dear Melissa,

If all has gone as planned, you are now sitting with Mr. Jack Rush and he is honoring my request to read this to you. He will soon be sharing with you an extraordinary story, one that is a part of your history. It was my wish and the wish of Mr. Blaine Duncan that our story should not die with us. As a direct descendent of this family, our story shall live on with you and it will be up to you to keep it alive as you see fit. You may remember your visit to Burkeshire Manor many years ago. It was then that I had the pleasure of meeting you, although I was not able to reveal my true identity at the time. Now you will learn the whole story.

With love and hope,
Penelope Whittier Burke

"I don't understand," Melissa said. "How could I have met her? She's been dead for hundreds of years."

"You will come to understand," Jack said. "This story began just over 60 years ago when I was only a boy of thirteen. In the end, only four of us knew the whole story. I'm the only one who remains now."

Jack began to tell the story of how he and Gabe Ingram had found the journal one summer. He told how they had read the journal and sworn to keep it a secret, waiting nearly thirty-two years to see if Blaine Duncan would actually come to Machias and buy the manor as the journal had said. He explained all of the references in the journal of how Blaine had traveled through time by no will of his own, to meet Penelope Burke. He gave the journal and letter to Melissa so that she could see these entries and the letter for herself.

Melissa noticed how the handwriting in the journal matched that in the letter Jack had read. "But this can't be," she said, more to herself than to Jack. "And what about the paintings she refers to?"

Jack smiled. "Come with me," he said.

Melissa put down the journal and followed him up the sweeping staircase to the master suite. He opened the door. "She created paintings for several of the many times they met," he said, pointing to the many paintings which covered the walls, "but not for all of his visits."

Melissa could see that the work was very old. Some of the paint had begun to chip away in places. But more than that,

248 | LEDA OSBORNE

she recognized Blaine Duncan in each painting as the man who had shown her the manor thirty years ago. She also recognized the woman whom she had known as Anna in most of the paintings.

"This is Penelope Burke," she said. "It's true. She was here that day, and I actually met her."

"There's more," Jack said as he led her back downstairs to the parlor. He went on to explain what had happened when Blaine was discovered at the manor that fateful day in May 1693. He gave Melissa the journal once again to read the account. Melissa read, her voice filled with awe as Penelope described how Blaine and the timekeeper had saved them from the fire and brought them to a future day to hide until Levi Burke's death 67 days later.

Jack stopped her at that point so that he could show her something more. He opened the box sitting nearby him and lifted out a pair of dresses. The style was very old and they looked damaged.

"You see," Jack said, holding the bottom of each skirt out for Melissa to see. "This is where they were scorched by the flames. This one belonged to Penelope, and this one to Chloe. These are the clothes they were wearing when the timekeeper brought them here. It was in those 67 days that you were able to meet your own great-grandmother. She told me about it the next day when I came. I remember that day very well."

He reached into a smaller box and pulled out some old

Polaroid snapshots. "You see, these are the pictures Blaine asked you to take of them."

Melissa looked at each picture as the memory of that day came rushing back.

Finally Jack explained the relationship that developed between himself and Chloe. "I never saw her again after the 67 days," he said sadly, "but Blaine continued to travel back. He and Penelope shared many years of love."

He sat without interrupting as Melissa read the remainder of the journal. When she had finished, there were tears in her eyes.

Jack sighed. "I am the last to know the story. Not too many years from now, I will be gone too. They did not want their story to die with them. Now it's up to you to keep it alive."

"So you have brought me here to tell me their story, and your story?"

"I have brought you here because this is now your story. The story of who your family was, and, because this all belongs to you now. Blaine had no children. This place belonged only to him in the present day and to your grandmother in the past. Now it belongs to you. That's what they wanted."

Melissa was stunned. Burkeshire Manor belonged to her. The once home of her great-grandmother. The setting of two incredible love stories. The place where time shifted like sand under the ocean waves. She felt unworthy of such a legacy. She barely knew her benefactors. But they were, indeed, her family. It was all so unbelievable, and yet, with the letter, the journal, the paintings and the memory of the woman she had met so many years ago, and the strong resemblance they had to one another, Melissa did believe. More than that, she knew in her heart it was true. She would keep their story alive. It was the least she could do.

"May I see their graves?" she asked.

"Of course."

Jack led her to the cemetery. He brought her first to Penelope Burke's grave. There were fresh red roses on it. Melissa touched the headstone tenderly. How remarkable to think that she had met her own great-grandmother, and yet here she was standing at a grave more than 200 years old.

Next, he brought her to Chloe's grave. It too, had fresh flowers. Here, it was Jack who touched the headstone with love and some sadness. Finally, he brought her to a double head-stone. One side was for Christina Duncan, the other side was for Blaine Duncan. Between them, the epitaph read:

WE ARE NOT DIMINISHED BY THE BREVITY OF OUR LIVES,
NOR ARE WE MADE LESS BY THE PASSAGE OF TIME,
BUT SHALL REMAIN ALWAYS AS WE WERE,
NO LESS, AND FOREVER.
PENELOPE WHITTIER BURKE

Melissa Sturgis kept her word to keep the story of Burkeshire Manor alive. She wrote and published a book describing the wondrous events that took place there, both past and present.

Burkeshire Manor became a legend to the generations that followed. The names of Penelope Whittier Burke, Blaine Michael Duncan, Chloe Dunnigan and Jack Rush would live on for all time.

There are many who say it is just a story, devised for effect, with no substance, but some of us know better. Fact or fable, I'll leave that up to you. But if you should ever find yourself in the midst of such a mystery, perhaps you will remember this story and know that time is only a perception, one that can be changed. And if you can conceive of such things, you may find yourself to be the next legend in the making.

Timothy Keeper

READER'S DISCUSSION GUIDE

The following questions may be useful to promote discussion among the members of your reading group.

1. Has your interest in the nature of time been stimulated by reading this book?

2. Did you share Blaine's frustration at the idea that events in your life may be foreordained, or did the revelation of time being omnipresent fill you with fascination as it did for Penelope?

3. Do you feel that foreordination of certain life events diminishes the value of those events? Why?

4. Are there other, formerly impossible, considerations concerning the nature of our existence which you now are willing to consider?

If you enjoyed stretching your imagination with The Timekeepers Tapestry, watch for **Searching For Mary,** coming soon. With the aid of her gifts of telepathy, a child psychologist, Julia Panelli, teams up with psychiatrist Marcus Sanders to find out who, exactly, is living in the mind of a young girl. Will they be able to free her before it's too late?

79670958R00157

Made in the USA
Lexington, KY
24 January 2018